THE BEST THINGS IN LIFE ARE DUKES

Dukes in Danger
Book 10

Emily E K Murdoch

ARE YOU SIGNED UP FOR DRAGONBLADE'S BLOG?

You'll get the latest news and information on exclusive giveaways, exclusive excerpts, coming releases, sales, free books, cover reveals and more.

Check out our complete list of authors, too!

No spam, no junk. That's a promise!

Sign Up Here

www.dragonbladepublishing.com

Dearest Reader;

Thank you for your support of a small press. At Dragonblade Publishing, we strive to bring you the highest quality Historical Romance from some of the best authors in the business. Without your support, there is no 'us', so we sincerely hope you adore these stories and find some new favorite authors along the way.

Happy Reading!

CEO, Dragonblade Publishing

Additional Dragonblade books by Author Emily E K Murdoch

Dukes in Danger Series
Don't Judge a Duke by His Cover (Book 1)
Strike While the Duke is Hot (Book 2)
The Duke is Mightier than the Sword (Book 3)
A Duke in Time Saves Nine (Book 4)
Every Duke Has His Price (Book 5)
Put Your Best Duke Forward (Book 6)
Where There's a Duke, There's a Way (Book 7)
Curiosity Killed the Duke (Book 8)
Play With Dukes, Get Burned (Book 9)
The Best Things in Life are Dukes (Book 10)

Twelve Days of Christmas
Twelve Drummers Drumming
Eleven Pipers Piping
Ten Lords a Leaping
Nine Ladies Dancing
Eight Maids a Milking
Seven Swans a Swimming
Six Geese a Laying
Five Gold Rings
Four Calling Birds
Three French Hens
Two Turtle Doves
A Partridge in a Pear Tree

The De Petras Saga
The Misplaced Husband (Book 1)
The Impoverished Dowry (Book 2)
The Contrary Debutante (Book 3)
The Determined Mistress (Book 4)
The Convenient Engagement (Book 5)

CHAPTER ONE

15 August, 1811

L UKE BEAUCHAMP, DUKE of Ashcott, absolutely knew he was not welcome. It was something a duke always knew, partly because it was so rare.

The invitation was clammy in his hands. Or was it his hands that were sweaty? Were his nerves so visible, his fear—

No, not fear. Anticipation. Fearful anticipation.

Luke cleared his throat as he entered. *He needed to pull himself together before he actually saw anyone,* he thought firmly, straightening up to his full height which was not inconsiderable. He pulled at the corners of his jacket and wished to goodness the hot weather had come any other day.

Not at a wedding.

It was a scandalous wedding, of course. Luke had read all about it in the gossip sheets, curiosity piqued. Scandal or not, however, it was a prestigious affair, and surely, she would be invited to such an event. She would be there—he would see her.

It was all the incentive he needed to demand his finest suit and visit the barber. He should have gone weeks ago, his hair had been getting far too long. But he'd had no reason to until he thought he might be seeing her again.

Lady Margaret Everleigh.

The hall was not busy. A few wedding guests chattered at the sides of the room, but it appeared the receiving line was in the drawing room. The happy couple stood, beaming at guests, beaming at each other.

Luke's heart wrenched.

It wasn't fair. That should be him. Him, and—

"There he is! No, not that one—there!"

"The Duke of Ashcott?"

"The greatest rake in the *ton*! What is he doing here?"

"I heard he'd seduced more than a hundred ladies in Paris alone."

Luke snorted. There probably weren't a hundred ladies in Paris alone that he could seduce, even if he had wanted to! But then, he had been the one to purposefully construct a persona of rakish devilry. He only had himself to blame if it came back to bite him on the—

"Good to see you, old chap!"

Someone was squeezing his elbow, hard. Luke looked up and saw the beaming face of Martock.

"I haven't seen you in polite company in months," Martock said happily. "Or in impolite company either, if it comes to that!"

He guffawed.

Luke glared. The hand on his shoulder, as expected, was now adorned with a gold band.

Was every duke in this place getting married off? Was he the only one miserable and alone?

Luke tried to take a deep breath. He was—what had old Penshaw called it? *Seeing shadows.* He was seeing shadows. Just because, as his dark gaze flickered around the room, a certain someone wasn't here—

"And I thought you were married by now!" continued Martock, clearly completely oblivious to the glower on Luke's brow. "Come now, a man like you, charming, rich—"

"Just declare my income, why don't you," growled Luke,

scowling around the room.

Too late. A few ladies of indistinguishable rank were looking over with great interest.

Blast.

How many times did he have to tell hopeful mamas and indignant papas, he was simply not interested in their daughters?

There was only one woman who appealed to him, and she was lost to him forever.

"Oh, got to go," said Martock, rapidly releasing him. "Looks like the wife wants to leave and—I mean, duty calls."

With a wink Luke tried to ignore, Martock rushed off toward a pretty-looking woman with a mischievous look in her eye.

Dear God, did they have to be so blatant! Why, everyone in the place could clearly guess what they were about to—

"Nora," coughed someone behind him.

"I beg your pardon?"

Luke turned. He wasn't aware of having offended anyone—at least, not sufficiently to require anyone to beg his pardon. Not today, at any rate.

Rakish reputation notwithstanding, he had left most of that life behind. What had been the point, after Lady Margaret—

"Ashcott," came the first voice in awe. "I . . . well, I did not expect the honor . . ."

Luke blinked and took in the scene before him. *Ah, yes. The happy couple.*

The bride was smiling at him in a knowing way, which boded well for old Thornfalcone—she didn't seem to be one who was easily overawed by a title. And she was elegant, far more elegant than he would have predicted—though Luke knew that was his old prejudice coming in.

If he was going to be anything different than his father—

Then he saw the look of genuine respect and deference in the bridegroom's eyes, and his heart sank.

Oh, yes. He had forgotten old Thornfalcone hadn't been born to inherit the title. There had been that brother of his, wasn't there—a lout, by all accounts. Luke had never encountered him.

But he had died, and now the younger brother had the title. That would explain the awe, the look of wonder at Luke's presence. The man respected him merely because he had been born a duke.

Well, Luke thought bitterly, *that didn't mean anything.* He'd been the biggest rogue in the *ton*. He'd lost everything.

Still, he had to put on the show. Everyone expected Luke Beauchamp, Duke of Ashcott to be a certain way, didn't they? Speak a certain way, stand in that imperious manner, treat people like they were nothing. It was an easy enough habit to slip back into, even if Luke hated it. He had to perform. He couldn't let anyone see the pain.

He shrugged as lazily as he could manage. "I was in the area, and thought I might see—but then, you do not know her. If you had known her, you would have invited her."

Oh, damn.

Immediately, Luke realized his mistake. He had let his guard down just an inch, and immediately his private thoughts about a certain woman had spilled from his lips.

No wonder the new Duchess of Thornfalcone was looking blankly at him.

Luke cursed himself, but it was too late. He had made himself a talking point. Again. Had there not been enough scandal when the engagement had been broken?

The Duke of Thornfalcone, on the other hand, clearly knew what he was talking about. Luke watched as embarrassment tinged his cheeks. "I am afraid—well, in truth, Your Grace, I did invite her."

Luke's heart leapt, but then just as swiftly sank back down. Did invite her . . . but evidently she had not come. Why not? Had Peggy known he would be here? Did she guess he would come just to see her?

"You invited her?" Luke could not help but ask. He had to clarify precisely what the man was saying. "And she did not come?"

"Her . . . well, her brother came," said Thornfalcone, tension in his voice. "Erm . . ."

Something lodged, hard and uncomfortable, in his throat.

Her brother. Henry.

Christ on a stick, that blackguard was here? He should have brought a pistol—no, Luke had promised himself last year he would not hold the brother accountable for his own mistakes.

Even if it had been Henry who—

"Ashcott," said a cold and painfully familiar voice.

Luke's jaw tightened as the Thornfalcones stared. Then they didn't know—at least, the duchess clearly knew nothing, and the duke only suspected.

No one knew the full story. Not really. He knew most of it, but there were still parts he didn't understand. Parts only Peg could explain. If she would ever agree to see him.

Knowing this would only cause him pain, and absolutely certain this conversation was not going to go well, Luke turned around.

His stomach twisted painfully as he beheld Henry Everleigh, Duke of Dulverton. *It was most unfair, Luke thought darkly, that the brother should have the same hair as the sister. And the same nose.*

Different eyes, though. No one had eyes like Peggy. Why, when viewed underneath the stars—

"I did not think you would be bold enough to come here," said Henry in clipped, plainly furious tones.

Luke chewed the inside of his cheek to prevent himself from responding immediately.

What the devil was the man talking about? It was a free country, and this was a wedding reception. He had been invited. The outrage, suggesting he was not welcome here!

Trying his best, however, to keep control of his growing temper, Luke bowed low. Far lower than he ever bowed to anyone. Anything to show Henry he had changed, that he could respect a gentleman as long as he earned it.

"Dulverton," he said quietly.

"And you'll notice that my sister is not here," said Henry curtly. "I am keeping her far away from you. You've done enough damage."

It was impossible to keep his face impassive. Luke attempted to speak calmly. "I promised her—"

"Your promises are worth nothing, and I do not want to hear them," Henry said coldly.

Luke flushed. The last thing he needed for this conversation was an audience, but the Thornfalcones were clearly agog, unable to turn away from the spectacle.

Dear God, that this was their next meeting! He hadn't seen Henry since that fateful night, when the man had come home early and discovered his sister and Luke—

Mary, the Duchess of Dulverton, placed a hand on his arm. "Henry, I think—"

"I think I should be going," said Luke stiffly. This had been a foolish idea—God knew what had got into him. *He needed to leave, now.* "Good day, Your Graces."

After a curt bow he turned on his heels and strode, head held high, out of the room.

Unfortunately he did not leave swiftly enough to avoid hearing the bride.

"Now what was all that about?"

And then he was out in the street in the baking hot sun, still holding the crumpled invitation and wishing he had never bothered to go. Luke breathed out a long sigh. Would that he could remove the tension from his shoulders as swiftly as he could the tension in his lungs.

Well, that had been a fiasco.

Not a disaster though. No, Luke thought as he started to walk back toward his townhouse and the safety of his own privacy. No, a disaster would have occurred if Peggy had been there. For all his fine ideas, for all his desire to see her after so long . . . what would he have said?

Luke groaned, sidestepping a governess with two unruly children, as he considered what words he may have spluttered in Peg's presence.

"I-I love you."

"I m-miss you."

"W-When we're apart I feel like I'm falling apart, literally disintegrating, like you were the only thing keeping me whole."

Luke rolled his eyes as he turned a corner at high speed. He would have sounded like a complete dolt, and he knew it.

No, better to avoid all that nonsense. Better to avoid baring his soul, breaking his mind, and completely berating those around him for even considering being happy.

The sun beat down relentlessly, and Luke hardly knew where the warmth from his own embarrassment and shame ended and where the heat from the sun began.

Either way, it was most uncomfortable. Luke ran a finger around his collar, wishing to goodness his valet hadn't made his cravat so tight. The sooner he could get home and out of this ridiculous attire—

"Ashcott!"

Luke sighed as he forced his feet to slow. What sort of duke would he be, after all, if he abandoned all sense of decorum and politeness?

A happier one, a cruel voice in the back of his mind muttered. *A much happier one.*

Plastering a smile upon his face, however, Luke paused and turned to see who had shouted his name.

His heart sank, though as it was such a frequent occurrence, he hardly noticed. *Of course. Wincham.*

The Duke of Wincham grinned. "Ashcott! You old dog, you haven't been seducing anyone, have you?"

Luke tried to smile, he really did.

He couldn't blame Wincham. Well, he could, but he probably shouldn't. It had been his reputation for so long, Luke wasn't surprised no one had noticed he had not touched a woman since—

He was not going to think about her, he thought and shook himself mentally. That was only going to lead to heartache, and he'd had plenty of that already. He was not going to think about Peggy . . .

Damn.

Luke swallowed, hoping his momentary pain had gone unnoticed by the other man.

"I hardly ever see you in Town these days," his friend was saying. "In fact I was talking to Gilroyd, and he said . . ."

Luke allowed the words to wash over him.

It was the same old thing anyway, he could almost recite it. If he were a particularly suspicious man, he would have wondered whether his friends were ganging up on him, all reading from the same script.

They were worried about him. They hadn't seen him out and about. They hadn't heard any outrageous stories about him, and they all knew he was a rake, a scoundrel, a seducer, so why hadn't he been raking and scoundreling and seducing?

And Luke would always smile and laugh, try to hint at dastardly deeds they hadn't heard about. All the while he would think about his time in France, and the love of a woman he had lost which had sent him there . . .

"I said, did you?"

Luke blinked. *Ah.* Evidently Wincham had deviated from the script this time. "I beg your pardon?"

Wincham grinned. "Thinking about her, are you?"

Luke did his best not to blanche, but it was a hard won thing to keep his face straight. He had not thought anyone in Society knew about Peggy.

At least, of course they knew *about* her. Lady Margaret Everleigh was one of the most eligible ladies in the *ton*. Everyone sought her hand at dances, everyone wished to sit beside her at dinner, everyone wished to play her at cards.

His pulse throbbed at his temple. *Of course they did. How could they not?*

"Her?" he asked vaguely.

"Whoever it is that you are seducing," Wincham said quite happily. "I don't bother attempting to keep up with all your scandals, there are simply too many. You need to settle down, man, get yourself a wife!"

Luke's taut jaw ensured his clenched smile did not waver.

They were back onto the same old lines then. He knew they couldn't depart for long.

Get himself a wife, indeed. As though it were that simple! As though one single broken engagement had not ruined him for all other women. As though he did not compare every young Miss he was introduced to against the perfection of Peg.

As though a man could kiss such a beauty and then forget her.

"I see," Luke said aloud, avoiding all commitment like the plague.

Wincham nodded sagely, as though he had suddenly become an expert in matrimony. "Yes, when I met my Hattie—but of course, you don't know that story!"

Luke shrugged. It hardly mattered whether he knew it or not. It was always the same: introduction across a crowded room, polite chitchat, her father would—

"Yes, she shouted at me most furiously when we first met," Wincham continued blithely, as though that were entirely normal. "And the second time she was wearing breeches, and I shouted at her—"

Luke blinked. He must have misheard. Surely Wincham had not said—

"In fact, I don't think I've cursed so much in front of a woman, you know," said his friend with a wry smile. "What a wife, eh?"

Utterly at sea, and unsure if he would catch up, Luke gave up trying to understand. "Indeed."

"Oh, marriage, you must try it, Ashcott!" Wincham continued. "Being so attuned to another person that you can sense their needs before they even voice them. Knowing you are seen and loved by another. Oh, there's nothing like it! In fact, when my darling . . ."

There was a burning sort of feeling bubbling in Luke's chest now. He knew precisely what it was, and it did not do him any service.

Envy.

What sort of a bachelor duke envied a married man? He should be gallivanting about, bedding as many women as possible, and boasting about it at the Dulverton Club, Luke knew.

Except he didn't want to. He wanted to end a long day at the fencing club and return home to the welcoming arms of his love. He wanted Peggy to smile when she saw him, share his bed, laugh at his terrible jokes.

Dear God, when had he got so sentimental?

Luke sighed. He knew precisely when.

He had played with Peggy's heart thinking his own immune, and when her brother had returned and thrown him out . . . well, it was only when he had lost her that Luke realized just what a jewel Peggy was.

"—a little one on the way!" Wincham ended proudly.

Luke waited expectantly for the rest of the sentence, but apparently that had been it. His friend was now looking at him with just as much expectancy.

Blast, what had the man been saying? Oh, right. A little one.

"Congratulations," Luke said with a brittle smile.

Wincham chuckled happily. "Can't believe it! The child has already been most disruptive, but I wouldn't swap it for the world. You should get married, man!"

"Being a duke is all that I need to be happy," Luke said in a harsh tone. "And I pity any man who is insufficient without a woman to make him look good."

It could have been the heat, the painful interaction with Henry, the agony of not seeing Peggy when he had to—Luke did not know. Perhaps it was some combination of the three, but Luke hated himself immediately for saying it.

The light died in his friend's eyes. A stiff awkwardness descended between them.

"Ah," said Wincham.

Honestly, what had possessed him? Apart from blinding envy and a terrible need to prove he was not lovesick, of course. Other than that.

"Well, I think you're a damned fool," said Wincham quietly. "And a lonely fool, and a half-crazed fool because you lost the woman you loved. Though I can appreciate how that would make a man less polite than he should be. I . . . I'll see you at the Dulverton Club, I'm sure."

And without another word, Wincham was gone, leaning heavily on his cane as he went.

Luke sighed, pulling a hand through his hair as he watched the man go. *Christ, they had been dependent on each other for a time in France.* It had been Wincham who had helped him out that time he was without a horse, and he had helped bring the brute home when Wincham had injured his leg.

And now he could treat him thus?

He needed to get home. *Home*, Luke thought, and the cool of the marble floor, and a cold bath, and an escape from the eyes of the world. He lifted a hand, and felt the presence of the letter which he had carried with him for many months now. It was still there.

Increasing his pace and wondering why he had not hailed a hansom cab to relieve him from this burdensome heat, Luke tried to think of nothing that had happened so far that day.

Not the irritating invitation that had only been delivered this morning.

Not the fear and hope he had felt in equal measure when he'd arrived.

Not the way he had looked about so desperately to see Peggy's dark curls.

Not the disgust her brother had treated him with.

Not—

He had turned a corner at high speed without looking, and something suddenly arrested his progress.

A sensation of sudden weight, of warmth, of a person—a body in his path. Soft skin, tantalizing curves, and the scent of peppermint and lemon entangled in it all.

And Luke was transported, just for a moment, to the past. To the Peggy he knew, the woman who had happily accepted his kisses, desired his embraces, perhaps even desired more though they had never gone any further.

And he blinked, and the world roared back into color, and there stood Lady Margaret Everleigh.

CHAPTER TWO

Peggy stared, her vision swimming in and out of focus. Because it couldn't be him. It couldn't be.

But as her eyes adjusted to the sudden loss of momentum, a tall man with dark hair and an all-too intelligent smile appeared before her.

Luke Beauchamp, Duke of Ashcott.

Emotion flooded through her, though exactly what sort, Peggy did not know. *Desire? Pain? Shame? Guilt?*

Perhaps a medley of all of them, and something else besides.

People were continuing past them on the street, hardly noticing she was staring up with shocked eyes at a man she had not seen for months. No, a year? Perhaps more than a year.

"Peggy," Luke breathed.

Peggy swallowed and took a step back. Unfortunately, thanks to her rather unexpected collision with the handsome duke which had quite literally knocked her breath out of her, she was disorientated. She did not step back along the pavement. She stepped into the wall.

"Ashcott," Peggy said, her mouth dry.

Oh, how she had hoped that if she were ever faced with such a dilemma her words would not fail her. She'd hoped she would be imperious, aloof, and most of all, quick witted.

Instead she was staring up at him, noticing the few additional lines around his eyes, the way silver was scattered around his temples, trying not to think of the last time she had seen him. The last time she had been truly happy.

It had been the sneeze that did it. Peggy was almost certain if Luke had not sneezed, her brother never would have guessed there was a gentleman hiding behind the curtain.

That was the benefit of the drawing room: the curtains were floor length. Perfectly designed to hide a man.

As it was, her brother Henry had returned home without a single note of warning, and Luke had only a moment to disappear behind the curtain. And when he sneezed, Peggy had been unable to keep her face calm.

She could still remember the brilliant flush which had scalded her cheeks. "Henry—"

"By God, you've got a man here," her brother had said, putting down his wine glass and glaring as though she had betrayed him.

"No, I haven't!" Peggy had lied.

And hadn't she betrayed him, in a way? After all, a duke demanded utter respect from those around him, and that meant his family had to be utterly beyond reproach.

Peggy had known that growing up, and it had never bothered her much. Why, naturally she was not going to permit herself to be tempted into a compromising position. No, she would find a match just as her mother had done. Through a matchmaker, to make her family happy. It had all seemed so simple.

Until she had met Luke.

"Margaret Everleigh, you tell me right this moment," Henry had said, pointing a warning finger at her.

And Peggy had leapt to her feet, unable to stop herself. She was a grown woman, and she was in love. A mere brother wasn't going to stop her! "You have no right to tell me what I should and shouldn't do. You've gadded about with your mistress no doubt for weeks and—"

It had been a low blow, but not beyond the realm of possibility—and as she watched her brother's face tinge, Peggy had been triumphant in her knowledge that she had been right.

"I have not—that is beside the point!" Henry had blustered.

In that moment, Peggy had been sure she could talk her brother around. After all, he was hardly a paragon of virtue, and Luke had that very evening offered her something she had never believed possible: his hand. A life with him, not just stolen kisses when no one else was watching, but his whole heart.

Her body had thrummed with the hope of what lay ahead. If she could only entreat her brother—

"Come out, you blackguard, so I can see you!" Henry had bellowed.

It was all Peggy could do not to look at the curtain. Was this the right time for Luke and Henry to meet? Could there be any other? Why, in just a few moments, Henry could be celebrating with them. It was an exciting new expansion of the Everleigh family.

Her spirits had leapt as Luke appeared from behind the curtain with a rueful look. Oh, had any gentleman ever looked so well? Had she ever doubted, even for a moment, that he would make her the happiest woman in the world?

"Sorry about the sneeze, old thing," Luke had said apologetically.

Peggy had smiled, fingers itching to slip between his own. Well, it wasn't what she had planned, but there it was. Sometimes you couldn't plan for complete happiness. Sometimes happiness found you.

"Sorry!"

She'd rolled her eyes at her brother's explosive utterance. Really, Henry was far too quick to anger. There was no need for him to be so dramatic.

"I wasn't actually apologizing to you," Luke had said stiffly. Peggy always loved that about him—how formal he was to others and how deliciously informal he was to her. "To Peg—"

"Don't you dare talk to my sister in that—that tone!" Henry had spat, stepping forward.

Peggy had swallowed. This was not how things were supposed to go. Henry was supposed to be surprised, yes, and perhaps even a little indignant he had not been consulted when it came to finding his sister's betrothed.

But there was real, genuine anger in her brother's eyes.

She had to do something—precisely what, Peggy was not sure. Oh, if only she'd had some warning Henry was coming home, she could have prepared Luke, prepared herself! As it was—

"You sir, are contemptible," Henry had growled. "And after dishonoring my sister—"

"Henry!" Peggy had grabbed his arm, trying to pull him back.

This was all going wrong—what did her brother think he was doing?

Besides, she was hardly dishonored. Society would be astonished to know she had been kissed, and quite thoroughly, too—but just by the man she was to marry. They had done nothing more.

And only because Luke had been too much of a gentleman, Peggy had thought wryly as she tried to pull Henry away from her beloved. She had been quite willing to allow Luke more, and she had been rather surprised to find he was far more old fashioned than she'd realized.

And in just a few weeks, they would meet at the altar and be together for the rest of their lives.

"You challenge me, sir?" Luke had said then, expression blackening.

Peggy's gaze had snapped from her brother to the man she loved.

What did Luke think he was saying? Challenge? A duel?

No, that was the sort of thing that happened years ago—decades ago! It was forbidden, illegal even, she was sure. And she could not have the two gentlemen most dear to her in the world engaged in such nonsense. One of them could be hurt!

But as Peggy had looked at Luke, she saw something she had never seen in his expression before. A defiance far stronger than sense, a resolve far greater than perception.

Her lungs had tightened. Just as she was about to speak, tell both men to calm down and talk like rational human beings—if they could manage it—Henry lowered his finger.

Peggy breathed a sigh of relief then as she released him. *Finally, some calm. Now—*

"No," Henry had said slowly. "No, but I want you gone— from London, from England."

The words rang in Peggy's ears.

"No, but I want you gone—from London, from England."

He wouldn't be so cruel. Luke wouldn't listen to him, why should he? He was aware of her affection for him, he would not—

"Dulverton," Luke had said quietly. "You do not know me, but I am the Duke of—"

"I wouldn't care if you were Prinny himself, I will not have gentlemen cavorting with my sister!" Henry blustered.

"Henry," Peggy had started, but it appeared her brother could not hear her.

"Be gone, and be grateful I have no pistol on me at present," Henry had said, chest heaving. "Go on."

Peggy had looked instinctively at Luke. He would understand her, even without her speaking the words—they were so attuned. He would know she wanted him to fight for her—needed him to, expected him to. He would not simply disappear. They had made promises to each other. This very evening, he had asked her to be his wife and she had said yes.

True, they had not told anyone of these promises. But would not Henry be the most suitable person to hear the news?

Peggy reached for Henry's arm, but this time to calm rather than restrain. He was going to be surprised once he heard, of course, but it would reassure him that Luke was not the blackguard he had evidently taken him for.

Then Luke did the unthinkable: he nodded. "As you wish."

He turned. As though in a nightmare, Peggy had watched him step toward the door.

Only one thought resounded in her mind. *He was leaving.*

"No—Ashcott, no!" Peggy stepped after him, but Luke had already been close to the door and as he walked through it, he had slammed it behind him.

It was the slam that broke her.

If Luke had merely shut the door, she would have understood. Perhaps he would have waited in the hall to explain precisely why he had not fought to be her husband when it had really mattered. Maybe he would have sent her a note, apologizing and repeating all the pretty promises he had whispered in her ear that evening.

But he had slammed it.

Peggy had not known Luke long, but she knew him well. He was not coming back. Despite everything he was to her, what she had thought she was to him, against the vow he had made mere minutes earlier . . . he had abandoned her. He had broken their engagement before it had really begun.

Peggy's arm had fallen from Henry's, falling listlessly to her side. "He's . . . he's gone."

And that had been the last time she had seen him—until now. Until this moment, on a street in Bath, when she had least expected it.

"Peggy," Luke repeated.

Peggy drew herself up. She had allowed herself to become momentarily lost in reflections of that evening. For a moment, she'd even believed she was in love with him again.

But she was not. Luke Beauchamp, Duke of Ashcott, had absolutely no hold over her anymore. Now all she had to do was prove it to him.

"I'm terribly sorry," she said as nonchalantly as she could. "I'm late. Goodbye."

Hopefully, she thought, *Luke could not see how rapidly her heart was thundering as she stepped around him and kept walking.*

Yes, that was all she had to do—keep walking. The man would soon get the hint and—

"Peggy!"

Peggy's pulse fluttered at the sound. She was not going to permit herself to even consider talking to him. What would it achieve? Apologies for making her love him? Apologies for not even attempting to win her brother over? No, she had put all that behind her and—

A hand on her arm. It burned.

Because of the heat of the day, Peggy thought, wrenching her arm from a man's touch which she had gladly welcomed last year.

"Excuse you," she said sternly to the tall Duke of Ashcott now walking alongside her, most irritatingly matching her stride. "You appear to have me confused with someone else."

"No," said Luke, that handsome smile she knew so well slipping across his lips. "You're Peg—"

"You have me confused with someone who wishes to speak with you," said Peggy crisply, almost relishing the instant impact her words had.

It was a strange sort of satisfaction, seeing Luke Beauchamp, Duke of Ashcott's face fall. There had been a time when she would have been mortified to create anything in him but joy.

That time was over. The sooner he learned to accept that, as she had, the better.

"You cannot mean that," Luke said quietly.

Peggy attempted to increase her pace, but the blasted man did not even seem to be breaking a sweat to keep pace with her.

Thankfully she was almost home. Then she could escape this—this whatever it was.

Oh, that they had to meet again in such a public place! Peggy could feel the curious eyes of all they passed along the street. Lady Margaret Everleigh, pursued by a gentleman?

The very idea!

"Go away," hissed Peggy under her breath.

"Not until you talk to me," he replied quietly.

"I have nothing to say," she muttered back. Well, nothing she could say aloud, at any rate.

"Peggy—"

"Don't call me that!" Peggy said, rounding on him and trying to catch her breath.

She had barely looked where she was going but that hardly mattered. She was staring up into the dark eyes of the most handsome man in England. At least, that's what she had thought when she had first laid eyes on him.

Oh, to go back and warn herself not to get involved with this treacherous duke!

"I-I am sorry. Lady Margaret," Luke said quietly.

Peggy blinked. *Now that, she had not expected.* Where was the bold and brash duke who had so winningly secured her affections? Where was the arrogant duke who had so proudly announced, only the third time they had met, he was going to—

Well. Her cheeks pinked at the mere memory of what he had suggested he was going to do. Ladies did not speak of such things. Ladies were not, as far as Peggy was aware, supposed to even think such things.

It had been difficult not to think of such things once Luke had mentioned them. It was difficult not to think of them now.

Peggy lifted her chin in defiance. *She was not going to allow this duke to get the best of her!*

"I don't want to talk to you," she said bluntly.

There was a look of shock, of real hurt in the duke's eyes. It was so surprising Peggy almost took a step back.

Why was he shocked? Had Luke not made his feelings abundantly clear when he had left, ignoring her completely and slamming the door behind him? Had not the silence which had grown between them over the months been sufficient enough a sign?

"Y-You don't?" Luke stammered.

Peggy could not help but stare. Where was the determined, arrogant man she knew? The man who had been so certain about everything, who would simply inform someone if their opinion was incorrect? Where was the Luke Beauchamp, Duke of Ashcott, she knew?

She swallowed. Perhaps it was best he was gone. That was the man she had fallen in love with, after all.

"I don't," she said succinctly. "Goodbye."

Yet again she was unable to step away. Not because of any lingering feelings. *They*, Peggy thought severely, *were over. Gone. Dead.* But because once again, the man had the audacity to grab her arm. And in public!

Peggy wrenched herself free and glared. "If my brother saw you doing that—"

"If your brother saw me doing that, he would see only a fraction of what I want to do to you," breathed Luke, somehow far closer than she had expected.

That he could say such a thing! Dear God, that he could mean it! What on earth was going on? Fractured understanding and pain were pouring through her and Peggy did not know what to do. Why was this happening? How could the man be so cruel?

Trying to ignore the pointed stares of those passing them on the pavement, Peggy hissed, "What are you playing at, Ashcott?"

"Playing at? Nothing, I just—"

"Because you've had months to do something, say something, anything!" she continued, hoping he could not sense the agony in her words. "Months! Over a year!"

A strange sort of crestfallen look came over the duke's face. "I know, but—"

"You could have said something that night! The night you broke—I mean, you almost broke my heart!" Peggy amended quickly.

The last thing she needed was for Luke to see just what an effect his betrayal had.

Not that it had. *She was almost completely past it,* Peggy

thought as she tried to take a deep breath. She hardly thought about him at all. She had almost returned to normal life. Almost.

Until today. Until an accidental meeting had her thinking again through every moment of that night.

"Why now?" Peggy asked quietly, the words slipping from her mouth before she could stop them. "Why, Luke?"

She had not meant to call him by his first name, and she saw a flicker of something cross the duke's face as she did so.

They had been so open, once. So unafraid to share their thoughts, so eager to embrace each other's feelings. They had shared a bond almost as close as that of man and wife, and if Henry had not turned up so unexpectedly, who knew? Maybe it would have been so.

Peggy took a deep, steadying breath.

But they had not. And worst of all, she was getting the exact same response to her question now as she had all those months ago. In short: nothing.

She could have been forgiven for hoping Luke was about to make a grand gesture, not a sweeping statement but a heartfelt, specific apology. Anything. Anything to make it clear he regretted what had happened that night.

Peggy was not sure what she would have done if he had. How could one respond to a love lost? How could you forgive such pain, pretend it had never occurred?

But as she looked up into Luke's face, she saw nothing, no passion, no apology, no desire to make things right. And she wasn't going to wait anymore. She'd done her waiting.

"Stay away from me," Peggy said coldly. "I never want to see you again."

As she turned on her heel and kept walking in the direction of home, a part of her—a very small part of her—hoped he would follow. That Luke would disregard her wishes, as he had so often done in such a charming way before, and follow her.

But no footsteps echoed behind her. No handsome gentleman came up beside her, matching her pace. No voice called her name, no hand appeared on her arm.

It was all she could do not to turn around. But she wouldn't.

Luke Beauchamp, Duke of Ashcott, was part of her past. Not her future.

CHAPTER THREE

16 August, 1811

IF IT WERE possible to crush a cobblestone with one's shoe, Luke would already have done so.

The cobbles themselves had done nothing to warrant such treatment. But for the last twenty minutes, he had stormed up and down the same street, the same pavement, muttering under his breath and drawing a great many concerned looks.

Eventually Luke steadied himself, planted his feet in one place, and glared up at the door he was now before as though it had betrayed him most grievously.

The door remained untroubled by the duke's ire.

Letting out a deep sigh that did nothing to distract from the tight feeling in his shoulders and the headache starting to brew at his left temple, Luke shook his head.

This was a mistake. He had known it would be before he'd even left his own house. But that did not seem to matter. The moment he had decided on this plan of action, he had done what he had always done: barreled toward it with no consideration of consequences.

And now he was standing outside Peggy's door with a bouquet of wilting flowers and an equally pathetic excuse.

"You're a fool, Ashcott," Luke muttered under his breath.

A woman passed him, raising an eyebrow. He bit down the instinct to call after her and say it wasn't his fault, but there was no point.

Besides, it was his fault, wasn't it?

Straightening up, Luke examined the knocker carefully, as though it were a cannonball which could be shot at him at any moment.

He was here to woo—no, that wasn't quite the right word. To court?

Dear God in His Heaven, you'd think a man of six and thirty would know how to go about this. But then, few of his . . . connections in the past had been particularly appropriate. None of them, in fact. Except her. Lady Margaret Everleigh.

Peggy.

Before he could stop himself, before he could second guess himself, before he could change his mind and storm back home in high dudgeon, Luke rapped the door knocker.

The door was opened so rapidly, he actually took a step backward in astonishment.

"Yes?" said the man pointedly.

Doing everything he could to gather his wits, Luke stared at the tall man. He himself was hardly short, but this individual was at least three inches taller. He was dressed in the Dulverton livery and had the presence of a man who was in charge.

The butler, then?

If so, he was a different man to that which Luke remembered. *But then,* he thought, *that had been over a year ago.* Maybe the old one had retired.

Or maybe, muttered an exasperated little voice in his head, *the Dulvertons have different staff in each of their homes. You wooed— almost seduced—Peggy in London. This is Bath. Try to keep up!*

Luke managed a weak smile. "Good afternoon. I—"

"Is it?" snapped the butler.

How did the Duke of Dulverton permit his butler to be so

rude?

For just a moment, Luke was so flabbergasted that his voice failed him, but he rallied as best he could as the roses in his hand continued to wilt. "Yes, I would say it is—"

"Well I wouldn't," said the butler with equal force. "Go away."

Luke's mouth actually fell open at this retort as the butler continued to glower down at him. *How dare a mere servant address him in this way?*

If only it weren't so hot, he thought as he wiped sweat from his brow with a handkerchief before stuffing it in a pocket. Then he'd be thinking clearly, and not keep straining to look past the butler into the hall. Just in case Peggy was there.

"How dare you, man!" Luke managed. "Speaking to me in that uncouth manner, what would your master say?"

"I think my master would give me a sovereign," came the outrageous reply.

Luke's eyes widened. He had never claimed to be a particularly proud member of the *ton*. Fashionable etiquette and dress passed him by, in the main. Even more so after he had left for France. But surely no duke would wish his butler to behave so.

And then the butler sniffed. "To think you believe I wouldn't know you, Your Grace!"

That was when Luke's hopes started to sink.

"All the Dulverton servants have been given strict instructions not to permit you into the house," said the butler blithely, looking Luke up and down as though he had committed a great crime. "I have your features memorized, Your Grace, and I will not permit you inside."

Luke wilted like the flowers in his hand. "You won't?"

The butler shook his head. "Not on your life, excusing the expression, Your Grace."

All the Dulverton servants? Taught what he looked like, perhaps given a sketch to memorize, all to prevent him from going through the door? The thought rushed around Luke's head, but it made less sense the longer he thought about it. Was he truly so repugnant that the entire house was barred to him?

No, this was ridiculous. He was a duke! Surely Dulverton would understand. *He may not like me*, Luke thought feverishly, *but he was a gentleman.* He would not be so uncouth as to completely deny him entry.

Would he?

"Look, all I want to do is have a chat with—"

"Lady Margaret is not at home," the butler said severely, gazing down his nose.

Luke swallowed. Well, of course he would say that! That was the oldest trick in the book! He wasn't going to be fooled by that sort of nonsense. Not at home, indeed!

"I demand—" he began stiffly.

"You don't get to make demands here," came a voice from behind the butler. "Or anywhere, if I have anything to do with it."

Well, he had tried. There was no point in continuing to push the point—not now the Duke of Dulverton had arrived.

And Henry Everleigh, Duke of Dulverton, looked just as angry as he had at the Thornfalcone wedding as he pushed aside his butler to glare at Luke.

"Demand was perhaps the incorrect word," said Luke slowly.

Try as he might, he could not marshal his thoughts.

Blast. He had not expected Dulverton to be home—which was ridiculous, now he came to think about it. The day was so hot, many of the *ton* had decided to stay in their homes until the air cleared. Lady Romeril was even threatening . . . promising to hold a garden party that did not start until nine o'clock in the evening! The idea that Dulverton would not be in his own house, when it was so intolerable to go elsewhere, had been foolish.

He should leave.

The instinct was so strong, Luke took a step back before he forced himself to still.

Leave? Now? He had come to see Peg—*to see Lady Margaret*, he adjusted swiftly in his mind, and he still wished to see her.

Longed to see her. Ached to—

"Stay away from me. I never want to see you again."

Luke swallowed. He had to make this right. Had to show her, explain his sudden abandonment of her in May of last year. By God, it had pained her just as much as it had pained him—it must have done.

His fingers tightened around the bouquet of roses. "Listen, Dulverton, I—"

"I have no interest in what you wish to say," said Dulverton airily, though his cheeks were reddening. "Do you think anything a lout like you could say would be meaningful to a man of honor like myself?"

Luke's jaw tightened. He was not a lout—well, no more than any other rake in Society. He hadn't left any woman with child, and he had paid off all his mistresses with good coin the moment he had tired of them. Not all gentlemen could say the same.

What he mustn't do, of course, was drop a genteel hint at the dishonorable way Dulverton himself had found his own bride. It wasn't polite to mention the working-class upbringing of the Duchess of Dulverton, and he was no such—

"A man of honor like you?" Luke found himself saying, temper rising. "You mean someone who permits his wife to get her hands dirty in a forge and refuses to let his sister think for herself?"

The words echoed around the hall before he could cram them back into his mouth, and he heard the butler gasp.

Dulverton's face remained impassive. "As I said. A lout."

Luke's cheeks burned, but he had no room to disagree.

Damn it all to hell, but he knew his tongue would get him into trouble again. Whenever he grew nervous, whenever he knew an important moment was approaching, what did he do?

Spout utter nonsense!

Shame and discomfort were trickling through his veins and Luke knew there was only one thing he could say. "I am sorry," he said stiffly. "It's just—"

"I think you have insulted myself, my wife, and my sister enough for today," said Dulverton smoothly. The calm façade cracked as he raised a finger. "And you would be a fortunate man indeed to be gifted the chance to see my wife in action in a forge! She has a true talent. Something you wouldn't know anything about."

Luke tried to take a deep breath.

Had two gentlemen ever seen less eye to eye? Had it ever been so impossible for a man to get a word in edgewise, fighting against both his opponent and his own nature?

Oh, Luke had always known he was a reckless man. He had been as a youth. But the older he got, the more damaging his impetuous behavior was becoming. After all, had he not stormed out of Dulverton's London drawing room when he and Peggy had been confronted? Hadn't he impulsively obeyed Dulverton's stricture to get out of the country?

Luke met the cold eyes of the man before him and wished to goodness he had acted differently. But that was then. All he could control, just about, was now.

"Dulverton," Luke said quietly. "I have no wish to quarrel."

The man snorted.

"I truly believe if we sit like gentlemen," persevered Luke, "converse like gentle—"

"But can you?" snapped Dulverton with a glare. "Our last conversation, the Thornfalcones wedding notwithstanding, was not particularly auspicious."

Luke's gaze flickered from the man before him to the hall beyond. Just a glimpse of Peggy would convince him to keep arguing with this blackguard. Just a hint of her dark hair, just a glance of her smile . . .

But the hall was empty.

"—unwelcome here, or any of my homes," the Duke of Dulverton was saying.

"I truly care about Peggy," said Luke, interrupting the man's flow. "About Lady Margaret," he added, seeing the look on her brother's face.

"I don't care if you care about her," Dulverton said with a frown.

Luke knew it was a bad idea to allow his emotions to over-rule him once again, but he could not help it. The irritation, the desperation to see her billowed up in him, and before he knew it, he was speaking once more with no filter on his tongue.

"Well, you might find that she does," he said bluntly. "Has it ever occurred to you, Dulverton, that you hurt your sister just as much as you hurt me by throwing me out of her life?"

It was, as ever, the wrong thing to say.

Dulverton glared. "How—how dare you—"

"I dare," snapped Luke. *Well, in for a penny, in for a pound.* "I dare because the only thing that matters to me in the world right now is your sister."

He'd never said the words aloud. Not to anyone, not even to himself. But as Luke said them, understanding dawned.

The only thing that he cared about, that truly mattered, was Peggy. He had to find her. If she truly was from home—

"If you cared about Peg," said Dulverton quietly, "why didn't you fight for her?"

And all the bluster, all the energy, seeped out of Luke's shoulders.

It was a fair question. A question he had asked himself time and time again, without discovering any real answer.

"You could have come to me, honorably, like a gentleman," continued Dulverton. "You could have asked my permission as her nearest male kin, and I would have said—"

"Absolutely not."

Luke turned toward the sound of the voice, and his spirits rose as the sun somehow poured down warmer onto his skin, because there stood—

Peggy.

She had not been at home then. The butler had not been lying. Wearing a beautiful light blue gown designed for visiting,

Lady Margaret Everleigh stood on the pavement, hands on hips, glaring at the two men.

Luke swallowed, but his throat was dry and it was impossible for him to make a sound.

How did the rest of the world continue as normal while Peggy was in it? How could all these people pass her by on the pavement without being caught by the radiance of her beauty? How did every gentleman who saw her not get down on bended knee?

You didn't, the treacherous voice at the back of his mind muttered.

That was because I was an idiot, Luke attempted to reply, his gaze unwavering from Peggy's glare. *I was a complete idiot, and it's only now I realize just what I've lost.*

Everything.

"Peggy," Luke croaked.

Peggy sniffed. "That's Lady Margaret to you."

Before he knew what was happening she strode past him, pushed him aside, and walked into the house. The very house he had been forbidden from entering.

Luke did not think. Thought was unnecessary at this point. His instincts knew precisely what he wanted: to be close to Peggy. He had to be close to her. If she entered the house, well, he would simply have to do so, as well.

He had forgotten about her brother.

"Oh no you don't!" said Dulverton harshly, pushing Luke back into the street.

But Luke was no longer willing to give up without a fight. Dulverton may be her brother, but he didn't know what was best for her—only *he* knew, truly knew, what she needed.

She couldn't be that different from the woman he had kissed all those months ago . . .

"Let me past!" Luke said gruffly, pushing against Dulverton and finding, to his surprise, that the man was far stronger than he looked.

Panic started to rise in him. He could still see Peggy, giving her bonnet and reticule to the butler, but at any moment she would go farther into the house and be lost from sight.

"Peggy!" Luke cried, desperation tinging every syllable. "Peggy—please, I must—"

"What you must do is no concern of mine," Peggy said calmly. She deigned to look at him now, but Luke could see only coldness in her eyes. "I don't want to see you."

"There you go," said Dulverton roughly, placing his hands on Luke's shoulders and attempting to push him back again. "She doesn't want to—"

"Please Peggy, I can explain!" Luke said urgently.

This couldn't be it—this couldn't be over. He had thought, time and time again, of how carefully he would reveal his affections to her. In privacy, in calm, in a drawing room somewhere, he would unfold his affections and she would finally understand how deeply he cared.

It wasn't supposed to be like this. Not two people wrestling in the doorway while the object of his affections refused to meet his eye.

His panic flared, giving him strength. Dulverton cried out with shock as Luke thrust him aside, and Peggy's eyes widened as Luke stepped forward to approach her.

"Peggy," he said, voice ragged from the effort. He stopped just a few feet away. Any closer, and he may lose his head and do something ridiculous. Like kiss her. "Th-These are for you."

Was his voice going to fail him once more?

He pushed the bouquet of roses into her unresisting hands. "Roses. For you."

Something joyful flickered as Peggy looked at them. The first step in reconciliation was—

Peggy held out the roses to the side without looking at them again, then opened her hand. They made a soft flumping noise on the marble floor.

"I don't accept roses—or any other flower—from rakes," she

said softly. Her fierce glare did not waver.

Luke swallowed. *Ah. Fine, so he had a little further to go with his apology—but he was here now, wasn't he?*

"You have to understand—" he began.

"No, *you* have to understand," Peggy said. "No, it's all right, Henry."

Luke glanced over his shoulder to see Dulverton approaching him with—was that a raised poker in his hand?

The duke lowered his arm with a glower. "Get on with it, Peg."

"I'm nearly done," she said lightly.

Fear rushed through Luke. "No, our conversation has only just begun—"

"I think you'll find it's almost finished," Peggy said blithely. "For I am finished with you. Understand me, Ashcott. There . . . there was something, once—"

Luke's spirits rose. She could not deny it, then, even with her brother looking on. Oh, the Peggy he knew and loved was still in there somewhere! Why could she not just accept that what had been between them was a fire which blazed too hot to be extinguished?

"—but that was a long time ago," continued Peggy, her glare still intact. "You lost any and all opportunity to court me. I am done with you."

Done with him? She couldn't be done with him! "I-I won't allow you to—"

All too late—again—Luke realized he had transgressed a line.

Fury flashed in Peggy's eyes, and as she took a menacing step toward him, Luke could do nothing but take a hasty step backward.

"You won't allow me? Oh, Luke Beauchamp, you credit yourself with far too much power and prestige. You are nothing! Nothing to me now," Peggy said, still advancing as Luke almost stumbled in his retreat. "And I think it is pathetic that you believe you can come here. That you believe a single bouquet of roses can make up for what you did!"

"I'll send you more bouquets," Luke said quickly, hope springing as his back foot met the threshold. "Hundreds of them, thousands—"

"You cannot solve a problem by throwing roses at it," Peggy said curtly.

Luke hesitated. How on earth had he managed to get here, back on the doorstep again? Peggy was standing before him in the doorway, and she almost looked—

His heart sank. *Pitying. Dear God, was it that bad?*

"I'm a duke!" he said desperately. "A duke!"

For anyone else, that may have worked. Luke hadn't. . . well, he had not used the title particularly, but it had never hurt. A woman never failed to be impressed by a title like "duke."

One did now.

Peggy raised an eyebrow. "Really? How fascinating. My father was a duke, my brother is a duke, half my friends are dukes. Is that supposed to impress me?"

The door slammed in Luke's face. A single rose petal drifted across the doorstep.

CHAPTER FOUR

17 August, 1811

PEGGY WAS GRATEFUL for the calming damp cloth on her brow, but she would have forgone it just to be alone. As it was . . .

"—absolutely disgraceful," came her sister-in-law's voice, hushed but not hushed enough, from the other side of the drawing room. "Why on earth did you let him in the house?"

"I didn't let him in!" That was Peggy's brother. His voice sounded sharp, upset. "The very last thing I wanted was for *this* to happen!"

Even without opening her eyes, Peggy knew precisely what he was doing. Henry was pointing.

In truth, it probably looked far worse than it was. While Henry had been blathering to their servants about opening doors to traitors and allowing rakes to even speak to Lady Margaret, Peggy had been . . . well, accosted wasn't quite the word.

Minny meant well.

But Peggy wouldn't have chosen to lie here on the chaise longue, with a cushion behind her head and a damp cloth across her forehead. She wasn't sick, after all.

Just lovesick, Peggy thought with a wry laugh. At least, she would have described herself that way a few months ago. Back then, she would have been desperate for five minutes alone with the man who had so swiftly won then abandoned her. Just to understand—if it were possible—*why*. Why had he made her love him then betrayed her? Why had he asked for her hand then just as swiftly walked away?

Her eyes under the damp cloth closed more tightly. That was then. This was now. Now, she had entirely rid her system of any interest in that man.

That man, who stood there as bold as brass, thrusting flowers at her!

And she certainly hadn't had any rather disobliging dreams in which the handsome Duke of Ashcott had showered her with roses . . .

Peggy cleared her throat as she sat up, damp cloth slipping to the floor, only to see both her brother and his wife glancing over with concern.

"Oh, Peg," said Henry with a sigh.

"You should lie down," said Minny, stepping to her. "Honestly, you must be—"

"I'm fine," said Peggy softly.

It did not seem to matter.

It was actually one of the things she had liked the most about her new sister-in-law. She had joined most of Society in being suspicious of Minny Banfield, the woman turning up at her home on the arm of Henry Everleigh, one of the most eligible bachelors of the *ton*. At first, Peggy had wondered just what kind of power this Minny woman had over her brother.

Time very swiftly proved that the hold was one of mutual affection, and sometimes the excruciatingly overt displays of said affection were too much to bear. Particularly after—

You are not going to think about him, Peggy scolded herself under Minny's chatter. You are not going to give a single thought to the man who had no real interest in you until he could not have you.

If that did not prove Luke Beauchamp, Duke of Ashcott to be a rake, she didn't know what did!

"—exerting herself by facing that brute," Minny was saying severely. "How could you, Henry?"

"It wasn't my fault!" Peggy's brother protested. "The man pushed past me—"

"You should have shut the door in his face the moment he appeared," Minny declared as she dropped heavily into an armchair. "It's outrageous!"

What was more outrageous, Peggy thought with growing concern, *was just how flushed her sister-in-law was looking.* It was a hot day, and any woman could be forgiven for being a little pink, but Minny Everleigh looked as though she were about to burst! Or at the very least, as though she were standing in her boiling forge. Peggy had visited her there once in the grounds of Dulverton Manor, and it had been sweltering, even in the depths of winter.

But the drawing room was north facing. Unfashionable in the winter, but a lifesaver in the summer. So why did Minny look so . . . so flustered?

"You mustn't exert yourself," said Henry in a low, concerned voice.

Before Peggy could say anything, her brother had quickly covered the distance across the room and was kneeling beside his wife.

"Oh Minny," he was saying fondly—so fondly that Peggy felt obliged to look away and wander to the window. "You must take better care of yourself."

There was such love in his words, Peggy was slightly embarrassed to be in the same room as them.

It had been the same just after their wedding. A short honeymoon had been cut even shorter, she recalled with a smile as she settled in the window seat, by the revelation that her sister-in-law was with child. They had returned, been insufferably happy, and had doted on little Henry the moment he'd been born.

Peggy had half thought they had finally got their fawning

over and done with, but the last fortnight it had started to become unbearable again.

She sighed, trying to ignore the whispers behind her as she watched carriages go by.

To find someone to share affection with like that—it was something she had dreamt of almost all her life. Once, she had thought she'd found it. *Ashcott had known how to whisper sweet nothings,* Peggy thought bitterly. He had far exceeded her expectations on that score. But it had been truly nothing. No true promise, no commitment, no matrimony.

Peggy traced a slight hairline crack in one of the small square panes of glass in the window.

Well, perhaps love wasn't going to be her lot in life. There were plenty of spinsters—*unmarried ladies,* she corrected herself. Many of them lived perfectly happy lives, from what she could see. And she was a lady. A duke's sister. *One day,* she thought with a twinge of pain, *a duke's aunt. Maiden aunt. Oh, Lord.*

"—careful with yourself, at all times but especially now," her brother was saying.

There was something in the way he spoke that made Peggy's ears prick up. "Why?"

She turned around and caught guilty expressions on both their faces.

Peggy frowned. "You . . . you're not . . ."

It would be most astonishing if Minny were. It was only a few months, after all, since little Henry had been born! Less than six months. Peggy was hardly an expert in these matters, but she had thought . . .

The looks of excited guilt and shared joy on the two Everleighs' faces before her, however, was more than enough to confirm her sudden suspicion.

Minny burst into tears and Peggy rose to her feet, hastening over to her—but once her sister-in-law started speaking, her concern lessened.

"I-I'm just so happy!" she sobbed, fat tears rolling down her cheeks. "An-An-Another b-baby!"

"We had decided not to tell anyone yet," Henry said with a wry smile as he placed a hand on his wife's shoulder. "A little early, we thought. We only became sure last week."

Peggy tried to smile and comfort the sobbing woman at the same time, though in truth, she was unsure whether Minny needed comforting. She'd been like this the first time, too. Anything—simply anything—could set the woman off. Henry said the record for the most ridiculous thing Minny had cried at was seeing a kitten fall over with tiredness. Peggy maintained it was looking at a ball of wool.

"Congratulations!" she said aloud to the happy couple.

Henry beamed and Minny sobbed harder than ever, a smile breaking through her tears, and Peggy did all she could to ensure a smile was plastered on her face.

So, Minny was once again with child. Her brother hadn't waited long, she couldn't help but think, before shuddering. Thankfully Henry was so preoccupied with his wife, he hadn't noticed.

Another Everleigh. Another child—something to absorb all Henry and Minny's attention, when it wasn't being spent on little Henry.

And their lives moved on, Peggy could not help but think with a sinking heart. They moved forward, their lives changed and expanded. And hers—hers stayed the same. Sadness mingled with her happiness for her brother and sister-in-law. In fact, her life was precisely the same as it was five years ago, now she came to think about it. It was not a very happy thought.

As their family grew, she just remained here, in the way. Far more in the way now she knew Minny was once again with child.

Peggy swallowed. She had put the letter aside when she had received it, believing she could think of nothing worse than accepting. But now . . .

"S-Sorry," sniffed Minny. She appeared to have drenched her handkerchief and was now dabbing her eyes with her husband's. "It's just—the emotions, I cannot express—"

"It's quite all right, Peg doesn't mind. Do you, Peg?" Henry said brightly.

Peggy widened her smile. "Not at all. But on the subject of change—"

"You've not received any proposals, have you?"

It was all Peggy could do not to wince at the excitement—and eagerness—in Minny's voice. Did she have to make it so obvious, how desperate they were for her to marry and move out?

"No," she conceded, trying to keep her voice light. "Other than a proposal from the Sedleys. They have invited me to their country estate for a house party, and I thought—"

"Oh, well you must go!" said Henry swiftly. Peggy met his eye and he smiled awkwardly. "That—that is, if you want to."

Peggy knew she was fortunate to have a brother like Henry. He was generous and thoughtful, sometimes foolishly so. He was taken advantage of by tradesmen and had somehow been coerced to pay fees for membership at the club named after their family— which their grandfather had founded!

But he was kind. And kindness was a quality, Peggy had discovered a long time ago, that covered a multitude of faults.

Still. If he could at least pretend to be devastated that she would be leaving their townhouse for a few weeks, that would not go amiss.

"We'll sorely feel your absence," Minny was saying. "Are you certain you wish to go? I never thought you liked the Sedleys that much."

It was unflattering of her sister-in-law to point that out, Peggy thought dryly, *but then she had been raised in an entirely different world.* Forges and blacksmiths, as far as she could make out, rarely needed tact.

"I barely know them," Peggy said aloud. "And what an excellent chance to rectify that error. I'll leave tomorrow."

"Tomorrow?"

"Tomorrow," she said decidedly, wondering if that would be soon enough to avoid a repeat of Luke's ridiculous display.

"Tomorrow I will be out of Bath and away from—I mean, visiting the Sedleys."

Peggy decided not to notice Henry and Minny exchanging glances. Let them think what they wanted. All *she* wanted to do was be away from Bath and in the cool of the country.

Which was why, when she found herself in a stifling carriage for several hours the next day, she rather wondered whether she had made a mistake.

After all, Minny was right—she had never liked the Sedleys much. Oh, the duchess was fine enough, but the way the duke carried on about France, and how to carry a blade, and secret codes! Anyone would think he was a spy!

And the carriage was roasting hot. No breeze entered the carriage windows, even after she tried to pull them down, and Peggy was presented with mile after mile of fields with nothing in the way to entertain.

By the time the carriage was rattling along a shadowy avenue that approached the Sedleys' home, giving her a few moments of cool, Peggy was determined to get out of the carriage, drink the largest glass of lemonade she had ever seen, and spend the next two weeks doing nothing but enjoying the country air. And, of course, speaking nonsense to the other guests, whomever they were. Not thinking of Luke Beauchamp, Duke of Ashcott, at all.

Which was why it was so astonishingly provoking, upon descending from her carriage, to see a very familiar figure standing in the shadow of the house with her.

"You!" Peggy blurted out.

Luke Beauchamp, Duke of Ashcott, turned. He was grinning.

"Hello!" he said cheerfully.

Peggy stared, hardly able to believe her eyes.

This was—no, she must be dreaming. It must have grown so warm in her carriage that she had drifted off. This was a dream— a nightmare. Luke couldn't be here! He was in Bath. She had come here to get away from the rake!

But as the crunch of gravel confirmed what her eyes were

telling her, that the blackguard was stepping toward her, Peggy could do nothing but stare at the handsome—at the irritating man.

This could not be happening. Her feet couldn't move. Her legs were shaking under her gown. How did the brute have this effect on her after all this time?

"Lady Margaret Everleigh," Luke said softly, under the noise of her coachman taking her trunks into the manor house. "Finally. A chance to talk."

And it was his ease of speaking to her, his triumph that he had somehow managed to get her away from the protection of her brother, that did it. Peggy glared, fury rising, and did something she had promised herself she would never do.

She touched Luke.

Well, it was more of a grab, really. Ignoring his startled cries, Peggy pulled the idiot by his jacket cuff until they had moved around to the side of the house out of view of the drive—and most importantly, the windows overlooking the drive.

Then she pushed him unexpectedly. To her delight, Luke entirely lost his balance, half falling, half crashing into the stone wall.

"Peggy, what—"

"How dare you!" she hissed under her breath, hoping to goodness her driver wouldn't hear. The last thing she needed was for the man to take tattle tales to her brother.

For some reason, the idiot looked rather surprised. "I thought you'd be pleased to see me!"

"Pleased!" Peggy's hiss had reached such a pitch, she hardly knew how she was creating it.

Only then did she notice she was still holding onto the man's cuff. Dropping it as though she had been seared, Peggy took a hasty step back. Thankfully, Luke did not follow her. He remained leaning against the wall, looking like—

Heat scalded Peggy's cheeks. Looking at her as though she were something to eat. *Oh God, what had she done to deserve this?*

"Yes, I thought—well, you clearly couldn't speak openly with your fool of a brother there," Luke was saying, as though she had any interest in listening. "And so I thought—"

"You thought I was not speaking my mind merely because Henry was there?" Peggy said in disbelief.

Had the man ever met her brother? He was a fluffy bunny. You could say anything you wanted before him, and he would simply nod if he agreed or flush if he disagreed. Henry wasn't the sort of person to censure her!

"You look well. Almost as beautiful as that card party we escaped, do you remember?" Luke's eyes were glittering with fond memories from the past. "I asked you if you'd ever—"

"And I said I had not," Peggy breathed. Then she came to her senses. "No amount of happy times recounted—"

"They were happy times, Peg, and I knew, if we could be alone—"

Peggy closed her eyes, just for a moment, in an attempt to gain her equilibrium. She had come to the Sedleys' to escape—to remove herself from Luke's presence in Bath. And now he was here. Her luggage was already inside, she couldn't retreat now.

Her eyes snapped open. Luke was still looking at her, a nervous grin on his face.

Retreat? She wouldn't give him the satisfaction. With any luck, there were a few others also invited whose company she would relish and she could avoid having cause to even speak to him for the entirety of her stay.

"I have no interest in being alone with you," Peggy said curtly.

Luke raised an eyebrow. "We're alone now."

"That's not the point—"

"And you were the one who dragged me around the side of the house, to be alone," he remarked, his second eyebrow rising. "Why, one would almost think you wanted—"

"Oh, be quiet," snapped Peggy.

Discomfort was circling inside her, coming to nestle in her

twisting stomach. The man simply did not seem to understand—and that was because, perhaps, she had always agreed with him when they had been . . . before. When they were something to each other that they could never be again.

Peggy drew herself up and tried not to notice how Luke's gaze flickered down to her chest. *Really!*

"I don't know why you're here," she began, in an icy a voice as possible. "But—"

"I'm here for you, of course," Luke interrupted with a swallow. "I'm following you. I'd follow you anywhere."

The blatant lie, cruel and heartless, tipped Peggy over the edge she was barely balancing on. Until that moment she had been certain she would be restrained, polite, and aloof. That was all he deserved, after all.

But after that?

"Follow you anywhere?" Peggy repeated in a quiet voice, tinged with repressed rage. "Anywhere? Luke Beauchamp, you didn't even stand still and ask my brother's permission for my hand when he gave you one cross word!"

The echoes of that moment were resounding in her mind, but she must not listen to them. Not if she was going to prevent herself from crying.

"Follow me anywhere—you disappeared from Town!" she continued. Her voice was breaking and she hated her weakness, but she knew that somehow she had to make him see. Luke finally had to understand what he had done to her. "You asked me to marry you then you disappeared from London! I couldn't find—I looked for you! I sent letters, and no one knew, and I . . ."

Peggy swallowed the tears as red-hot pain seared across her shoulders. It was debasing, to be this open, but she could see no alternative. Luke was staring at her with something akin to horror, but she couldn't stop now. This had to be done. Once and for all.

"You hurt me in a way I did not believe it possible for a person to be hurt," Peggy said, some of the passion disappearing from her voice. "I have never been so altered, and I think—no, I know, I will never be the same again. You broke me, Luke. You killed the woman I was. I'll never look at you with affection again, and you are fortunate indeed that I can look at you at all."

"Peggy—"

"Lady Margaret," she hissed, narrowing her eyes and wishing she did not find the man before her so ridiculously attractive. "It's Lady Margaret to you, and it always will be! Do not think this fortnight will be a chance for you to redeem yourself in my eyes. In my opinion, you are irredeemable. Replaceable. But not redeemable."

Peggy turned on her heel, hardly knowing where she was going but knowing she had to walk away. Luke. He was so . . . so intoxicating. Even when standing there, berating him, there was something in her that wanted to tip forward and fall into his arms. Be caught by him, held by him, kissed by him—

"Peg—Margaret!"

Peggy turned on her heel, bittersweet agony pinching at her heart as she saw Luke's astonished and rather upset expression.

Well. Finally. Now perhaps he could start to understand what it was to feel utterly betrayed by someone you cared about.

Not that he cared for her—how could he? If he had cared for her, truly loved her as he had said, would he not have stayed? Stayed for her?

"I have nothing more to say to you," Peggy said as grandly as she could manage, holding her head high. "Stay away from me. Approach me after this house party and I shall give you the Cut."

Luke's lopsided grin was nervous. "Not with a sword, I hope?"

Peggy glowered. "Don't tempt me."

CHAPTER FIVE

19 August, 1811

Luke almost tripped down the last step—but then, he had
done so every other time he walked down the Sedleys' large,
sweeping staircase, as well. It was twice as deep as the others, and
caught him with every descent. He supposed he should attempt
to learn to lunge.

He glared over his shoulder at the offending step and listened
to the silence.

That was the pleasant thing about being one of the earliest to
rise in a large house party. Oh, the other guests were fine enough.
Some of them were even charming. Perhaps if his affections
already hadn't been stolen by a rather dashingly beautiful, raven-
haired woman who hadn't stopped glaring since he had arrived,
he would pursue one of them.

As it was, however . . .

*"Do not think this fortnight will be a chance for you to redeem
yourself in my eyes. In my opinion, you are irredeemable. Replaceable.
But not redeemable."*

The silence was starting to become deafening. Oppressive.

The large hall's marble floor had been muffled decades ago by
copious rugs, so barely a sound echoed around it as Luke stepped

forward.

Well, it was another hour or two until breakfast. The gong wouldn't ring until ten o'clock. That left him time to investigate the reputation of this library Sedley simply wouldn't stop going on about. It was on the left, here, wasn't it?

Luke swept a hand through his hair as he opened the door. Yes, reading, that's what he needed. The opportunity to lose himself in a book, in someone else's life. Someone else's misery. Nothing else could distract him from—

The sound of a book hitting the carpet. A gasp. A hurried step back. The scent of peppermint.

"What are you doing here?" asked a rather dashingly beautiful, raven-haired woman.

Well, he could not have planned this better if he'd tried! There stood Peggy, mouth gaping, book clearly having just fallen from her hands. She was alone in the library.

Not alone. Not anymore.

"Peg—Lady Margaret," Luke swiftly amended.

Blast, it was taking all his concentration to ensure he called her by the staid, formal name he had long ago abandoned. It was most unfair that he therefore had almost no self-control left to prevent him from staring at the beauty who stood before him.

She was dressed, as one would expect, in a plain day gown—though in truth, nothing Peggy wore looked plain for long. This sea green gown floated elegantly over her shoulders, past her waist, to the floor.

Covering, Luke was certain, a multitude of pleasures.

He swallowed. Not that *that* was all he was interested in. Though he'd be a liar if he said he hadn't wondered how the curves and swells the gown suggested actually looked, once the muslin gown was removed and—

"Go away," said Peggy sternly.

Luke's astonishment at his own good fortune faded away. *Ah. Yes.* She wasn't particularly in the mind to listen to him, not after yesterday's rather hurried and mortifying speech.

"You broke me, Luke. You killed the woman I was. I'll never look at you with affection again, and you are fortunate indeed that I can look at you at all."

Shame and guilt roared through his veins, and he was unable to push aside the tremendously upsetting sensation that he had erred.

He had known Peggy was angry. He had already seen the anger—seen it in her brother too, which was far more threatening.

But to see her so hurt, so pained. To hear her speak of agony. Of how she would never be the same again. To know that it was his actions, no one else's, that had caused such pain . . .

Luke was far too proud to admit he had cried himself to sleep last night. No one would guess it either. He had been as debonair as he could manage at dinner, far too quizzical and charming for anyone to think his heart had been touched.

But it had. Not just touched, but wrenched out of his chest, stomped on, and left lifeless on the drive when Peggy had walked from him yesterday afternoon.

Luke swallowed. Not that he could explain that. Not yet. Not until she was ready to listen.

"Well, if you won't do the gentlemanly thing and go away, I suppose I shall I have to leave," sniffed Peggy, drawing herself up. "The outrage! Forced from a library!"

Luke did not entirely know what made him do it. It wasn't a conscious thought. It wasn't a plan. He hadn't even known that she'd been in there.

But now he had stumbled upon her, he would be a fool to miss the opportunity.

He took a step back, not taking his gaze from Peggy. His hand found the door handle.

"Thank you," said Peggy curtly, stepping forward. She obviously thought he was going to widen the door for her.

She could not have been more wrong.

Luke stepped back again. The door shut behind him and he

leaned against it.

Peggy's eyes widened. "What the—"

"I-I want to have a talk," said Luke, hating his voice had tremored right at the moment when he wanted to be calm.

This sort of opportunity was not one he would find again. Manufacturing it, indeed, would be impossible.

After she had been so open, so vulnerable with him yesterday, perhaps it was time to be similarly open with her. *After all,* Luke thought feverishly as Peggy frowned, *did she not have the right to know how similarly broken he had become?* How he regretted, had regretted for months, the way he had behaved?

That he was no longer the rake she and Society took him for?

"Am I a prisoner here?"

Luke stifled a laugh. That was one of the things he loved so much about Peggy. She was always so dramatic. "No, I—"

"Then let me out," Peggy demanded. "Honestly—the cheek!"

"I want you to listen," said Luke, words tumbling from his lips. He could see from the growing irritation in Peggy's brow that she would not listen for long. "Peggy, I—oh, by Jove."

"By Jove indeed," Peggy said. "I thought I told you—"

"Yes, yes, Lady Margaret," said Luke. *Perhaps humor would lighten the mood?* "Though how you expect a man to call a woman he's kissed by such a formal name—"

"Oh, is this a common problem for you?" Peggy's eyes flashed. "You poor thing."

Luke winced.

Blast it all, couldn't she see he was trying to be amusing? Though now he thought about it, the phrasing did have rather the flavor of a scoundrel. Damn it all to—

"I've got to get out of here," Peggy was muttering under her breath. She had taken a step away, eyes flickering around the room.

Luke knew what she was looking for. But the Sedleys' library only had the one door, and he was standing right before it— between her and the way out.

Guilt prickled his soul. It was not a very gentlemanly thing to do, certainly. If he heard tell of a man who refused to permit a woman to leave his presence, he would have described the man as a complete ruffian.

Strange, how swiftly one's morals altered when it came to one's own situation.

"I need to tell you—"

"I don't want to hear it," snapped Peggy, turning from him.

Bitterness rose in Luke's chest. Did she truly think she was the only one hurt by their broken engagement? "You don't even know what I'm going to say yet!"

"Whatever it is, whatever you think is important to say, is by definition something in which I have no interest," Peggy said to a bookcase. "I have become so dulled to your charm, Ashcott, what little charm there is—"

Luke swallowed his retort and allowed her to continue. *Lord knew, the woman had earned the right to vent.*

"—and am now entirely indifferent to you," Peggy continued.

He snorted. "Bit of a change of tune from yesterday, isn't it?"

That got her attention. Peggy turned, cheeks blazing red, hands curled into fists. "I should never have—I misspoke yesterday."

And just when Luke thought he could not be further bruised, she managed it.

She misspoke? All those feelings which had poured out of her, the very real sting he had seen in her eyes . . . it was not true?

Luke did not know what was worse. He had felt awful hearing of her suffering, knowing he had been the creator of it. But in a way, hearing she had not spoken the truth, that he had not touched her affections was an equal agony. All he wanted was for her to love him. Now she was trying to argue he did not affect her at all?

Balderdash.

"Anyway, I do not understand why you are keeping me here," said Peggy, lifting her chin in an imperious manner that reminded Luke powerfully of her brother. "You clearly have no feelings for me, or you would not have done what you did."

Luke opened his mouth, hesitated, then closed it. He should have prepared this speech—but then he had not expected to find here in the goddamn library! He had thought himself free from all company for at least an hour, in which he could have prepared something—something far more eloquent than what this was going to be.

He sighed and tried to push his shoulders back and chest out. That was the best way to generate confidence, his father had always said. When a boy was as shy as Luke, while being the heir to the Dukedom of Ashcott, a father had to teach his son some tricks.

The trouble was, Luke could not help but feeling the tricks had done rather too good a job. The whole of Society thought him a scoundrel, a rake, and he was.

But he wasn't.

"Peg—Lady Margaret." *Damn.* "When I proposed marriage all those months ago—"

"Four hundred and sixty-five days."

Luke stared. *How on earth . . .*

Peggy's cheeks reddened. "But who's counting?"

"You are, apparently."

This was all going wrong—he needed to concentrate on his feelings. On how embarrassed he had been to be discovered by Dulverton, how he had meant to come back the next day, but his pride—oh, his damned pride.

Luke cleared his throat. *Fine. Here goes.* "When I proposed marriage, I—I meant it. I loved you."

"Well, if that is how you treat someone you love, I would hate to see how you treat those you disdain," said Peggy dryly.

Did she say these things purposely to torment him? Luke took a step forward and saw with surprise that Peggy stood her ground.

So, she didn't mind if he came closer, did she? Interesting.

He was sure there was a part of her, though how large a part he did not know, that still loved him, ached for his touch, wanted an explanation. Would swiftly fly back to his arms if she could be shown that he knew just how much of a mistake his abandonment of her had been.

The trouble was, Luke's tongue seemed to be tying itself in knots rather than giving that explanation.

"I'm not perfect," he said testily.

"Obviously."

"But neither are you!" Luke said before he could stop himself and regretted the words the moment they left his lips. Blast it all to hell. Perhaps if he gave her the letter—

Peggy raised an eyebrow. "I cannot tell—is this an apology, a confession, or a criticism of my character?"

All three, Luke wanted to say, but he managed to restrain himself. "I don't believe falling in love should make you ignorant of a person's faults."

"Nor restrain you from listing them, it appears," said Peggy bitterly. "Oh, go away, Ashcott! What good can this do?"

It was a question Luke was starting to ask himself. He had thought, coming to the Sedleys' house party would give him abundant opportunities to have a sincere and direct conversation with Peggy. And in a way, he had been right.

But being in her presence, breathing her in, seeing the way her cheeks pinked whenever she looked at him was enough to drive any man to distraction, let alone a man who had already broken an engagement with her. A man who knew how those lips tasted. Knew how soft that skin really was.

"Stop it."

Luke blinked. "I beg your pardon?"

Peggy's face was a picture of embarrassment. "Whatever y-you're thinking, stop it."

So, she could see the desire on his face, could she? Did she know just how much he craved her? How her laughter rang in his dreams, her joy deepening his anguish?

Luke sighed heavily. *Try again, man. She's worth it.* "I should never have left that night, and I should have come back the next morning. But my feelings . . . the way I felt, the way I feel about you . . ."

Why was it so impossible to get the words out?

He strode away from the door toward a bookcase, as though grasping onto something real would make the pain in his chest dissipate. Luke half expected Peggy to rush for the door now that it was unguarded, but she did not move. She was watching him as though transfixed. As though his inability to speak was hypnotizing.

Luke closed his eyes. Perhaps that would make this easier. "Feeling about you, the way I felt, when I felt the feelings . . ."

His voice trailed away again, but that did not leave them in silence.

Much to his chagrin, Peggy was laughing.

"If you cannot even explain the feelings you purport to feel," she said coldly, "I doubt they were of much merit."

Luke had crashed his fist into the bookcase before he knew what he was doing. "Damn it, woman! It's their very strength that makes them impossible to articulate!"

A noise—voices, in the hall. Others were getting up now for breakfast. At any moment they could be interrupted.

The knowledge caused panic, frustration, and shame to once again course through Luke. Panic that he could be disturbed before this conversation could be concluded. Frustration that he had wasted so much time. Shame that he had once again degraded himself in Peggy's eyes.

That degradation, surely, could be the only reason for the way she was looking at him.

"Strength?" she said softly, pushing a dark curl from her eyes. "You want to talk about strength? How about holding your head up high in Society when everyone knows, somehow, that the greatest rake in the *ton* proposed matrimony then immediately rescinded that offer?"

Luke's stomach dropped. *Surely not—he had never heard of such a rumor!*

But he had left almost immediately for France, hadn't he? He'd abandoned London and the pain it held and hoped service to the Crown would be a suitable distraction. It had been, for a while. Until the memory of Peggy's face had pulled him inexorably back.

"Let's talk about the strength to continue attending balls, and card parties, and dinners, while knowing every conversation is about you," Peggy said quietly, her gaze not leaving his. "Knowing every swiftly stopped muttering is about you. Every pitying look is for you."

Every word she spoke was stabbing a knife further into his gut. How had he never thought of this? *How*, Luke thought viciously, *had it never even occurred to him?*

He may have left England with a broken heart. But Peggy had remained, forced to attempt to heal under the eye of Society.

Perhaps he really was a rogue.

"I don't want you to try . . . try whatever this is, anymore," said Peggy sadly.

Luke's head jerked up. "What do you mean?"

"Coming here, accosting me yesterday—"

"You were the one who accosted me!" he pointed out.

"Whatever," said Peggy dismissively. "Forcing me to listen to your speeches in this library, and you don't even seem to know what you're saying!"

She always did have a way of seeing right through him. Luke knew, if he could just show her how much he cared, things would surely be different. But she was right. This couldn't continue. Not like this.

"I'll give you a minute, nothing more, for your final words," said Peggy stiffly. "Go on."

Luke blinked. "What, now?"

"You were the one in such a hurry to make speeches," Peggy said, tapping her foot.

He could feel the irritation rising up again, sparking across his shoulders, clenching around his brain. What kind of chance was this to explain? She had to know it was no chance at all.

"You'd think you'd be pleased!" Luke said, his temper finally getting the better of him. He knew he'd wish to take back these words once they were spoken, too, but he was sore pushed. "Most ladies would be absolutely thrilled, a duke trying to woo them!"

"Is that what this is? Wooing?" Peggy looked astonished.

Luke took a step toward her and felt his pulse quicken with every inch he closed between them. "Yes—badly, I admit! I am not a practiced wooer, Peggy, because—"

"Don't call me that!"

"I'll call you anything I want," Luke growled.

They were mere inches away. Peggy's breathing was rapid, but it was nothing to the shortness of his own. Oh, if he could just kiss her, kiss away the fury, the pain, the memories of what had been—

"You're not wooing me, you're arguing with me," Peggy breathed, eyes bright. "Arguing with me about how I feel, as if you know!"

"I'm a duke trying to tell you—"

"And perhaps I would be impressed," she interrupted, her voice low. "Perhaps any other duke would impress me, but it's you, Ashcott. It's you, and I am not impressed."

Luke took a step back.

There was such coldness in her words. As though they had never been anything to each other. As though he had not taught her how to kiss, and she had not taught him how to stroke just behind her ear to make her shiver.

As though he had not offered her the world, his world. Everything that he was.

As though she had not accepted.

Luke swallowed. "I . . . I don't know what to say."

Peggy was breathing deeply, as though she had run a great

distance. *Perhaps they had,* Luke thought wildly. They had certainly covered a lot of ground.

"Fine."

The word slipped from his lips with regret, but he spoke it nonetheless. He was out of ideas, out of options, out of time. The breakfast gong had just rung. The breakfast room was just to the left of the library. Luke could hear the scraping of chairs, the pouring of tea, the excited early morning chatter that typified a house party.

He'd had his chance. And he'd wasted it.

"Fine?" Peggy repeated.

Luke nodded, his head heavy—but not nearly so heavy as his soul. "Fine. If that's what you want—if you want me to stop wooing you—fine."

"I wouldn't call it wooing—"

"Whatever you call it!" Luke said, taking another step away from the woman he loved. "I won't be pursuing you anymore. I vow not to pursue you."

For some strange reason, there was a look of confusion in Peggy's eyes. "You do?"

Luke nodded. It would hurt, every minute they were here at the house party—but he wouldn't allow harsh words to chase him away. Not this time.

No, this time Peggy would get her wish, and he would stay. Perhaps this time she would change her mind and send him away. Perhaps that would be best. But Luke's stubborn nature would not permit it. He was not going to retreat. Not again.

"Breakfast?" he asked quietly.

Peggy's face was a picture of perplexity. "You . . . you vow not to pursue me?"

"What—having second thoughts?" Luke teased softly.

It was the wrong thing to say. As ever. Peggy drew herself up and fixed him with a determined stare. "Not at all. Merely relieved you've finally given up on a hopeless cause."

CHAPTER SIX

20 August, 1811

PEGGY STARED AT the frazzled scrambled eggs on her plate.

"So nutritious, Cook tells me," the Duchess of Sedley was saying. "So invigorating, as well! I hardly have my eggs any other way now!"

Peggy attempted to get the scrambled egg mess onto her fork. Almost all of it crumbled into ashes through the tongs. What was left . . . well.

"So delicious," said the Duke of Sedley cheerfully. "I don't know why we didn't do it sooner!"

Smiling and hoping no one was going to ask her why she wasn't eating her scrambled eggs, Peggy kept her eyes averted.

There were six guests at the Sedleys', aside from herself and Ashcott. She had refused to speak to him since yesterday's altercation in the library, one which she had not been able to stop thinking about.

"Perhaps any other duke would impress me, but it's you, Ashcott. It's you, and I am not impressed."

Six guests, she thought, firmly turning her attention.

Miss Yates was a puzzling sort. Very pretty, very polite, but very . . . aloof wasn't quite the right word, but Peggy could not think of a better. She had barely exchanged four words with her, and left the connection feeling she had been charmed, but did not really understand how.

Then there were the Marnions. Mr. And Mrs. Marnion were good sorts, as far as Peggy could tell, and their son was quiet and a tad reserved, but she could see no ill in him. At almost one and twenty, it would soon be time for him to come into his majority. Perhaps that was why Miss Yates kept glancing at him down the breakfast table.

And then there were the two bachelors. A Lord Braedon, a viscount who had a very easy air about him but constantly told inappropriate jokes. And a Lord Castor, another viscount. He was quieter, more stoic.

In fact, Peggy had not thought much of him until this morning when he had sat beside her at the breakfast table.

"Good morning, Lady Margaret."

Peggy had smiled blandly. Ashcott had just walked in and, finding that the two seats either side of her were taken, had sat directly opposite.

She vibrated with annoyance, but there was nothing she could do. It would be the height of bad manners to ask him to move, and the height of scandal if she were to move herself.

Besides, he had promised, hadn't he? Ashcott had made a vow, one that had surprised her and pained her in equal measure.

"You . . . you vow not to pursue me?"

"What—having second thoughts?"

Whether he would keep his word was anyone's guess.

Peggy sipped her tea and wondered how she would get rid of her eggs. The trouble was, getting rid of things she had no desire nor use for was not something she excelled at. After all, there was the Duke of Ashcott, for a perfect example. Looking at her from across the table.

It was impossible to explain just how infuriating it was to have the man there. Peggy had thought, after his declaration he would no longer be pursuing her, that he would leave her alone.

There must be someone in this place he can seduce, she found herself thinking. *A maid or something.*

The thought flashed across her mind just as a jealous ache settled in her stomach.

Coincidence, Peggy thought. That was all.

Why should she care the man she loved—once loved, that was the important thing to remember—had tried to confess his feelings and utterly failed? Why did it matter that she had been trapped, momentarily, in a library and he had not even tried to touch her?

It was nothing to her. *He was nothing to her.* And just as soon as this house party was over, she would never have to see him again.

She ignored the pang in her stomach. She was hungry, that was all.

Looking once more at the crisped eggs, she sighed gently. She doubted they would be able to help with her hunger pangs.

"Oh, just ignore him, he's a devil for snaffling at food," the Duke of Sedley said cheerfully as a large black dog wandered into the breakfast room. "Just push him away, that's it."

It appeared all the other guests were eager to please their hosts. That, or they actually liked the breakfast served to them. Peggy watched as the handsome dog meandered around the breakfast table, sniffing eagerly at each lap, and was immediately pushed away.

By the time he had reached her, she'd had an idea.

"Here you go," Peggy whispered.

Encouraging the dog under the table, it did not take much for her to scoop the vast majority of the disgusting scrambled eggs onto her spoon. The spoon disappeared into her lap. When it emerged a few seconds later, the egg had inexplicably disappeared too.

"How are you liking your eggs, Lady Margaret?" Ashcott asked coldly.

Peggy's gaze jerked up, and she narrowed her eyes at his

irritatingly calm expression.

Really! Was the man purposely attempting to ensure she insulted their hosts?

"Oh, yes, how do you like them, Lady Margaret?" the Duchess of Sedley asked eagerly. "If you like them, I can send you home with the recipe for your cook!"

Peggy's eyes glanced at the remains of the overcooked concoction on her plate before she looked up at her hostess. The dog had meandered off in search of another willing victim. She was safe. "I find myself supremely impressed. Please, ask your housekeeper to slip a note into my luggage."

It was a genteel, calm, and polite response. It had everything in it, in short, that was expected of a woman of her rank.

So why, Peggy wondered, *did it rankle so much that she had been maneuvered by that rogue?*

"I have to admit, they don't suit my taste at all," came a quiet voice.

Peggy turned.

Lord Castor had a faint smile on his face and a distinct glint in his eye. "But I think you agree with me, Lady Margaret. And I think you, unlike the gentleman over there, are far too polite for your own good."

Relief washed over Peggy. It wasn't just the camaraderie of knowing she wasn't the only one to find the Duchess of Sedley's eggs repellent. That, she could have borne. No, it was hearing him criticize, albeit delicately, the Duke of Ashcott.

Peggy glanced over and saw with delight that Ashcott's cheeks were red.

How delightful! Well, at least there was someone at the breakfast table she could speak with to distract her from the infuriating man opposite.

"Far be it for me to criticize the way another woman manages her table," Peggy said in an undertone to Lord Castor. "It is not how I would do it, but this is not my home."

"I suppose you run your home far differently," said the viscount with a smile.

Peggy's own smile faded, just slightly.

When it had been just her and Henry, she'd had free reign to organize his household how she'd liked, and so she had. It was pleasant, to hold the chatelaine and always know your beef would be cooked to your precise specifications.

That had all changed, of course.

Not that she had anything against Minny. Of all the sisters-in-law she could have had, Minny was the dearest she could have hoped for—an absolute dream. She liked her beef cooked the same way as Peggy, for a start. But it was Minny's home now. Not hers.

"I have upset you."

"What—no, no, you have not upset me," said Peggy hastily, blinking. Lord Castor had a wry smile on his face. "I was merely—I was thinking of . . . it doesn't matter."

Out of the corner of her eye, she could see a certain gentleman appeared to be rather interested in her conversation with the viscount.

The handsome viscount, now she came to think about it. Peggy had hardly noticed when they had first been introduced two days ago. Now she looked at him properly, she would have to admit he was very well put together. In a tidy sort of way.

"I suppose you are the same," Peggy said with a smile. "You prefer the way you order your house above anyone's that you visit."

"Oh, I don't know about that—I have very little to do with the running of my house, in truth," said Lord Castor with a twinkle in his eye. "I have a rather marvelous housekeeper, Mrs. Reynolds, who supplies all my deficiencies."

Peggy laughed. Ashcott cleared his throat.

Well, well. She had only chosen to entertain Lord Castor's conversation as a method of distracting herself from the grumpy Duke of Ashcott. Now, it appeared, it had a rather unexpected secondary consequence.

It annoyed him.

Peggy could not understand particularly why this knowledge pleased her. She had never expected to be the sort of person who reveled in another's discomfort, but this wasn't just any old person. It was Ashcott. And as he had gone far out of his way to discomfort her—*coming here in the first place!*—why should she not make him a little discomforted in turn?

She smiled at Lord Castor and was rewarded by the sight, just out of the corner of her eye, of Ashcott's hand clenching around his teacup. Clenching so tightly, in fact, she could see his knuckles whiten.

Peggy felt a flicker of something that took her a moment to identify.

Was this what it was like, to have power over a man? To see that each one of your movements, however slight they may be, had an impact?

This had never happened before. Oh, she was aware she had some beauty, and her name and dowry had always ensured "Lady Margaret Everleigh" was invited to the right places. But to have a man so easily twisted into knots, to see that a mere smile given to another would make him so . . . so whatever this was?

It was intoxicating.

Peggy licked her bottom lip and was astonished to see not one, but two men shiver.

The Duke of Ashcott . . . and the Lord Castor.

When she and Ashcott had been—well, it wasn't courting, but whatever it was—it had always been Luke who held the power. She had been dazzled by him, outshone by him in every scenario. She had craved him, longed for any drop of attention he would pay her. If he had asked her to strip off all her clothes and give herself to him, Peggy had known she would have.

But he had left her, and she had learned to live without him.

He, apparently, had not.

"Lady Margaret?"

Peggy blinked. It appeared Lord Castor had been attempting

to get her attention. She turned to him and smiled. There was a clearing of a throat on the opposite side of the table. Her smile widened.

"I wondered how long you have known the Sedleys," said Lord Castor, as though he could not hear the muttering opposite them.

Peggy shrugged as gracefully as she could. "Not as long as I would like. I knew the duke first, of course."

"Friend of your brother?"

She nodded as she turned to pick up her teacup. Her gaze flickered around the table, taking in the Marnions arguing over the right length of time to steep one's tea, their son talking happily to Lord Braedon who appeared very bored of whatever topic it was.

And Ashcott.

He was glaring. He wasn't even attempting to hide it!

A shiver of pleasure snaked up Peggy's spine.

How had she never realized the delight in having power over a gentleman? Power over any gentleman of course would be pleasant, but over Ashcott?

"Friend of mine, in fact," she replied to Lord Castor. "I have a great many friends who are dukes. But not all of them."

And that was enough, it seemed. "More fool you!"

"I beg your pardon?" asked Castor curiously, looking over.

"Oh, ignore him," said Peggy, waving a hand and wondering how she was going to manage to drink her tea whilst feeling this giddy. "Tell me, Lord Castor—"

"Please," he said in a low voice, "call me Castor."

There was the sound of a man spluttering into his tea, but Peggy ignored him. She did not, despite great temptation, look away from Lord Castor who was looking at her . . . well, as Ashcott had once looked at her. As though she was intriguing, and beautiful, and worthy of notice.

A strange warmth was pooling between her legs, but it only increased when Peggy turned to place her teacup down and caught Ashcott's eye.

He was furious. That much was clear. The man had never been one to hide his emotions. It had been one of the things Peggy had liked about him at one time.

In this moment, she could see he was . . . oh, a number of things. Plainly furious with her, and angry at himself, and disposed to violently rip Lord Castor from limb to limb, she suspected.

The heat between her legs smoldered as Peggy beheld him. *Breakfast at the Sedleys' was not supposed to be so invigorating,* she thought with a smile. It shouldn't make her feel this alive, as though every inch of her body were tingling with bliss.

The trouble was, and Peggy hated to admit it even to herself, it was not Lord Castor's rather overt attentions that were melting her so thoroughly.

No. It was Ashcott's response.

His anger, his possessive nature which she had never seen before. That was the spark igniting in her bones. That was what was making her burn.

"Lady Margaret?"

Once again her thoughts had diverted far from her breakfast companion. With just a touch of guilt, Peggy turned once again to the viscount.

"I am sorry, Castor, I was momentarily distracted. It will not happen again," she said clearly. She was rewarded by a sniff from Ashcott. "You were telling me how long you have known the Sedleys."

And he told her. Peggy knew he did, because his mouth was moving and noise was coming out. Precisely what words he was using, and what they meant, she did not know.

How could she, when every iota of her concentration was focused on the man just visible in the corner of her eye? A dark man with a darkening brow. A handsome man whose features were splattered with jealousy.

No, Peggy amended. *It was envy.* Jealousy suggested he had some sort of right over her. Which he did not. Most definitely not. Luke Beauchamp had lost that right a long time ago.

"—and so of course, we have remained friends ever since," finished Castor.

Peggy smiled. "How lovely."

A grunt from the other side of the table was roundly ignored by both of them.

He was rather handsome, Peggy thought as Castor continued talking. The viscount, that was. She knew how handsome Ashcott was. She didn't need reminding.

And it wasn't wrong, what she was doing. She truly was enjoying his company and his conversation. Whatever it was. She was hardly making any promises, was she? It was not a crime to talk to a charming man at breakfast. In company.

The thought was unfortunately insufficient to prevent a slight pang of guilt.

This wasn't wrong, Peggy thought desperately. *It was hardly even flirting!*

"Peg—damn. Lady Margaret."

And that was the reward. Peggy felt a rush of triumph that far surpassed any guilt as she studiously ignored Ashcott.

Why this should please her so much, she did not know. Had she not told the infuriating man just yesterday when he had accosted her and trapped her with him in the library, that she had no wish to speak with him? That she had, in fact, no desire to hear his words of affection ever again?

"I don't want you to try . . . try whatever this is, anymore."

It had all seemed so simple yesterday. Yet Peggy did not understand the emotions flooding her now, nor why it gave her such a thrill to see the man so stymied.

"Lady Margaret."

"I—ahem. I think His Grace wishes to speak with you," said Lord Castor with a smile.

Peggy returned it, and did not turn around to look at the Duke of Ashcott. "I am sure he does. But I am talking to you."

"Damn it, Peggy—"

"And if he had any sense of respect," Peggy said, not bothering to raise her voice for she was certain Ashcott was listening to every word, "then he would know not to call me that."

A sudden crash—a noise she had not expected and which made her jump.

Not only her, it appeared. The entirety of the breakfast table started, a few of the ladies placing hands on their chests at the shock.

It was only then Peggy saw it was not quite the entirety of the breakfast table who had been startled.

Ashcott had risen from his seat so swiftly, it appeared, his chair had actually fallen back and toppled over. The chairback against the hardwood floor had created a resounding crash yet he stood there, staring, as though *she* had been the one to create the ruckus.

Peggy tried to keep her chin high and her gaze bold as she silently met the angry look of Ashcott.

"Dear me, what—"

"Are you quite all right, Your Grace?"

Ashcott did not respond to the words of concern thrown about the breakfast table. That is, he did not respond with words.

With a growl so animalistic, it caused a shiver of something Peggy could not quite name to flicker through her body, Ashcott stormed out of the breakfast room. He did not even bother to close the door behind him.

"My word," said Lord Castor quietly. "What a strange man."

Peggy tried to smile. It was rather strange—but what was even stranger still was just how alive seeing his anger had made her feel.

Best she did not investigate that particular thought.

CHAPTER SEVEN

21 August, 1811

H E SHOULD HAVE left half an hour ago.

Luke had never recalled a luncheon taking so long. Though he supposed this chatter, this lingering in their chairs in the shade of a large beech tree wasn't quite luncheon. The little sandwiches cut into triangles had been consumed, the lemonade had almost run out—thanks to Mr. Marnion—and there wasn't a single strawberry left.

And yet they were all lingering.

It was maddening. Luke could feel impatience tingling through his body, making him tap his foot as though that would hurry them all along.

After all, they surely couldn't intend to just sit here? All afternoon?

But apparently they did. Young Mr. Marnion was having a very interesting discussion, apparently, with Lord Braedon. The Duchess of Sedley was arguing genteelly with Mrs. Marnion about the state of modistes in Bath in comparison to Brighton. Everyone else was listening attentively, as though they could not conceive of anything more invigorating than . . . sitting down, listening.

Luke did not understand it.

He had never thought of himself as a particularly energetic person before. Surely he was like most people and did not like to sit aimlessly for hours on end. That was normal!

Yet here he appeared to be in the minority.

Despite himself, despite all his best intentions, Luke's gaze flicked just to his left. To Peggy.

Perhaps if she had not been so distracted, she may have noticed him. Felt the tenderness on the back of her neck. Turned to look at him, lips parted . . .

Luke cleared his throat. *Foolish.* That's what he was. Foolish. Because—

"Oh, Lord Castor, you are so witty!" came Peggy's melodious voice.

Luke's fingers tightened around the napkin in his grip. She was just saying that to annoy him, he tried to convince himself. To make him look the fool. Make him feel the fool. Well, he could make himself look the fool quite without her interference!

Wait. No, that wasn't right.

Luke sighed heavily. There was no breeze this late summer day and the sun was unbearable. Though they were all seated in the shade, it provided little relief.

He could hear a bumblebee somewhere, lazily humming as it drifted drunkenly from one flower to the next.

If he were to suddenly rise to his feet and storm off, there would be talk. Luke knew it. He would have to wait for one of their hosts to indicate they were free to meander. Glancing at both the duke and the duchess, however, he saw there were in no hurry.

"—never met a woman who understood it quite like you," murmured a low, fawning voice.

Luke snorted.

That man! That Lord Castor, whoever he was. The nonsense that he spouted!

Fine, Peggy was particularly brilliant—but he had known that long before this interloper.

"I think it'll be over soon," said Mr. Marnion impressively.

Luke glanced over, his bad temper seeping over. "What?"

His snap did not appear to distinguish the gentleman's certainty. Mr. Marnion smiled. "Why, the Frenchies, of course! They'll soon be begging us to come and free them from the tyrant!"

There was a murmur of assent from his son and one just after from his wife which made Luke smile. They clearly had no idea what they were about, Mr. Marnion even less.

Well, it was not his responsibility to educate people. These gentlefolk had no idea what it was like in France—no idea at all. And he wasn't going to waste his time trying to explain.

"I think you are wrong there," said Sedley smoothly.

All eyes flickered over to the duke, including Luke's.

Now that was interesting.

Oh, he knew old Sedley as well as he knew most people. Luke had not been raised to freely share thoughts or, heaven forbid, feelings, and neither would he embarrass any well-bred gentleman by asking him to do so. But that meant that, though he knew a few details about his host, he had never inquired delicately whether the man knew . . . well, about France. He had to assume not—dukes did not regularly risk their lives to do something as foolish as go to a war-torn country and spy there.

No, Luke thought ruefully. But that was the sort of foolish thing *he* had done, right after breaking off his minutes-long engagement with the woman sitting just there, smiling at another.

And it was not his place to try to convince these relative strangers about what was really going on across the water. So few people seemed bothered these days, anyway. France had been in the newspapers so long, there appeared to be a general malaise in the *ton* about the whole thing. It was rarely spoken of, and when it was, it was done incorrectly.

Luke shifted uncomfortably in his chair. The last thing he wanted was to reveal too much about his own exploits in that country, but it was going to be difficult to listen to such nonsense.

And the nonsense seemed determined to continue.

"—in my view," said Mr. Marnion impressively, as though he were an expert. "I have studied the matter, spoken with a great many people. I even conversed with an admiral just the other day, and everything he said agreed precisely with what I thought. And many agree—"

"I am not sure that I do," said a calm, gentle voice.

Luke almost fell out of his chair.

Was that—that could not have been Peggy?

Evidently he was not alone in his surprise. The entire party had turned to look at Peggy, or Lady Margaret Everleigh, as they would consider her. Miss Yates had a rather astonished look on her face.

Even Lord Castor looked surprised. "Goodness, don't you?"

Luke watched him whisper the words to Peggy, almost as though they were intimately acquainted.

The blackguard.

Oh, Luke had no evidence he was a blackguard, save for the fact that he was seated so close to Peggy, he had actually taken the liberty of resting his arm along the back of her chair.

The impudence!

"Y-You don't agree, Lady Margaret?" stammered Mr. Marnion.

Luke hid a smile by pretending to wipe his mouth with his crumpled napkin.

Well, this put the gentleman in a bit of a pickle, didn't it? Typically a gentleman would give way to a lady in all matters, particularly on something as trivial as this—and moreover, Peggy was above him in rank. Significantly above him.

But Luke could see by the continuing reddening of his cheeks that Mr. Marnion considered his knowledge on France as a point of personal merit.

This was going to be interesting.

"Yes, I think there are important movements on the Continent that make things in France rather nebulous at present," Peggy said calmly, a small smile lifting the corners of her lips.

Luke almost dropped his napkin.

Since when did Peggy have such an acute understanding of what was going on in the world—let alone in France?

"You—you do?"

Peggy nodded sagely, as though entirely unaware she was causing such a stir. Mrs. Marnion had gone red, the Duchess of Sedley appeared to be laughing, and as for Miss Yates . . .

Luke sighed.

Evidently a woman with her own mind and opinions was not something to be borne, even by the members of her own sex. It was most outrageous, of course. But there it was. It had always been so, and it would always be.

"I think I am correct in saying the war on the sea will be far more decisive than the war on land," Peggy said calmly, as though she wasn't disrupting all of Society's expectations of ladies in one fell swoop. "I believe the loss of the HMS *Minotaur* will be felt quite sorely by the Admiralty, but then I believe there are strides to be taken toward Paris which may render such a loss immaterial."

Pride warmed Luke from the inside out. *She was magnificent.* Surely there could not be found in the whole of England a more impressive woman. How she managed to go about the world without being proposed to left, right, and center, he had no idea. If he had his way they'd be married tomorrow.

"—have a marvelous mind," Castor was saying in a low voice, but just loud enough to carry. "I have never known a lady to take such an interest, Lady Margaret."

Luke's fingers clenched the seat of his chair. Why did this— this *boy* have to attempt to butter up Peggy like that? She was not a simpering miss, just waiting to be praised.

"Oh, Castor!" Peggy said, tapping the man on the chest as her cheeks pinked. "You are far too kind!"

Luke's jaw tightened, causing a sudden pain to shoot across

his temple.

That was not the Peggy he knew. The Peggy he knew would have rolled her eyes at the attempted compliment, demonstrated she knew far more than this idiot about everything, then walked off in search of better company.

And yet now she stayed. She laughed, her eyelashes fluttering.

It was enough to drive a man to distraction.

"Well, I think I shall go for a late afternoon ride," said Sedley in the silence, evidently feeling the conversation about France had run its course. "Will anyone join me?"

Finally, the luncheon party was breaking up.

Luke took the opportunity to rise swiftly, and in the medley of people rising to their feet, dusting off crumbs, and wondering aloud whether it was too hot for the ladies to ride with the men, he grabbed an arm.

"What the—"

"Come with me," he said quietly.

It was to her credit that Peggy did not throw a fit and shame him for taking her hand. She would have been well within her rights, Luke knew. After all they had shared . . . well, after the very little they had shared just the last few days at the Sedleys, she had every reason to refuse him.

But with pink cheeks and downcast eyes she allowed Luke to pull her along the hedgerow, then into what appeared to be a herb garden. Mingled scents wafted on the slow summer breeze, intoxicating Luke even more than Peggy's presence managed to do. And that was saying something.

The moment they were out of sight of the other guests, Peggy pulled her hand away. "You have some audacity."

"How did you know?" Luke said urgently.

Peggy raised an eyebrow. "Well, it's called good manners, you see. You may not have heard of them—"

"Not that," Luke said, cursing the fact she was always so much swifter than he was when it came to wit. He was known throughout Society as a droll gentleman, but when it came to Peggy, he felt a complete dunce. "I meant all those details about France."

He had not expected it to be a shameful question. It was simple curiosity which had driven him to ask it in the first place, to ignore all her previous requests that she leave him alone.

But despite the innocent nature of his inquiry, Peggy's cheeks colored rapidly. "I-I don't really, I just—"

"There are men in the army right now, men in Whitehall this very moment, who know and understand less about the situation in France than you do," Luke said sharply, heart fluttering painfully. "How do you know so much?"

It wasn't possible, was it? Well, to be fair he hardly knew Dulverton. He didn't strike Luke as the sort of man who would risk his own skin to serve his country, but even Luke had to admit his opinion of the man was rather colored.

It was even more outrageous to think that Peggy . . .

"I . . . I don't want to tell you."

Luke's gaze sharpened. He took in Peggy's clasped hands, the way her shoulders were slumped, the cringing cheeks.

Once, she had been more open with him than anyone in the world. She had told him so, revealed how comfortable she felt around him. Peggy had shared with him her dreams for the future, dreams of a home, a life with a husband who adored her, and children.

And now, Luke realized with a sinking feeling, *she did not even feel safe enough with him to tell him which newspapers she had been reading.*

Oh God, what had he done?

"Then don't," he said simply.

Peggy's eyes narrowed. "Don't?"

"I'm not one to force a woman to do anything—I'm not nearly so much a brute as you think I am," Luke added, unable to help himself. "If you don't want to tell me, well, that's your business."

He had half turned. Where he would go, he did not know. Luke certainly had no wish to go riding in this weather, no matter what Sedley said. Perhaps the library would be cool by this portion of the day.

His meandering thoughts meant he had stepped away, and so he was a few feet away when he halted at Peggy's words.

"It was . . . it was because of you."

Luke very slowly turned on the spot.

Peggy's cheeks still blazed red, but her shoulders had risen. She was defiant now, as though daring him to laugh.

Luke did not dare. "Because of me?"

It didn't make sense. What did she mean? Apparently she could read his confusion on his features, for Peggy sighed and looked at her hands.

"When Henry—when he told you to leave, to go to France, I . . . well, I inquired, and no one in London knew where you had gone, and so I thought: France. That was what Henry said."

"I want you gone—from London, from England."

Luke could barely think.

Peggy smiled sheepishly at her hands. "And so I followed the news. Every newspaper I could get my hands on, the lists, anything the Admiralty published. I thought, eventually, I would see your name. I would see you praised for your valor or—or God forbid . . ."

Her voice trailed away as Luke's stomach lurched.

She had followed the news of France only because she'd guessed—didn't know, merely guessed—he was there. And she did so in the full knowledge that the only mentions of him would be glory or death.

Luke swallowed. She was a far braver woman than he had ever given her credit for, and he had thought her brave when he had first met her. Across a crowded room. The music playing Mozart, the wine in his hand spiced, and he had seen a woman with brilliant eyes and a smile he had wanted to earn.

"I thought, even if you didn't know I still cared," said Peggy, her voice breaking as she looked up and met his eye. "I would know."

"You thought that?" Luke breathed.

She was defiant. "I loved you, Luke. For a long time. We had good times, laughter—"

"The apples we filched from the Duke of Axwick."

Peggy's eyes glittered. "That was your idea."

"You were the one who hid them in your skirts."

"It was the best excuse I could think of," she murmured. "For you going anywhere near my skirts."

And that was what did it. Not the knowledge that she had followed the news, not the way she had impressed with her information in the luncheon party. Not only that she had put her own peace and happiness in harm's way, waiting day after day for the news of his death, a death she must have thought was inevitable. Luke knew now that despite his betrayal, despite his sudden absence from Town, Peggy had forced herself to read those newspapers, day after day, waiting for the worst news a person could get.

No, it was because she still remembered the good times. The flirting. The way it had felt like they were magnets, and when they were drawn inexplicably from each other, it was physically painful to hold his distance.

Actual thought never entered into it. He did not need to think. The instinct was too strong.

Before either he or Peggy could say anything, Luke had closed the distance between them and pulled her into his arms.

He could have wept as his lips met hers. It was like the whole world had been put to rights, finally, after months of everything being wrong. As though no time had passed at all.

Peggy was motionless in his arms for an instant, but within a breath she had melted. Her lips parted, allowing Luke in, welcoming him with her tongue and an ardor that scorched them both.

She was his, and he was hers. His Peggy. His everything.

Luke's hands were gripping her waist but hers were moving, and he moaned into the kiss as Peggy's fingers entwined around his neck, and—

And then it was over.

Peggy staggered backward, lips plumped by his kiss.

Luke smiled weakly. "Peggy, I—"

"That—that was a mistake," she said swiftly.

All the joy, all the rightness Luke had felt, seeped away. "A mistake?"

Confusion dripped from every syllable. *How could it be a mistake?* They were made for each other, meant to be together. Had not their escapades last year proven that? Had it not been clear to the world? Had the Society gossips not spoken, almost daily, of their impending marriage as the only thing that would salvage their reputations?

"You had your chance," Peggy said, taking another step back before turning, as though to return to the beech tree. "Now . . . now it's Lord Castor's turn."

Luke snorted, following her through the hedged archway back onto the lawn. "You aren't actually considering him as a prospect, are you?"

The thought was ridiculous. A terrible jest that managed to sour his stomach and irritate him at the same time.

Peggy was just a few steps ahead of him but they were in view of the rest of the house party now. He could not reach out and take her hand, slow her, for fear of being seen.

Luke almost laughed again. *Fear of being seen?* They had not been afraid of being seen a year ago. The whole world could have watched him pay court to Lady Margaret Everleigh for all he cared. What did it matter who knew the woman he loved? But now—

"Peggy—damn it, Margaret," Luke said, quickening his pace to see her face. "You aren't seriously considering that idiot as a candidate for your hand? Are you?"

The defiance in her face was more than enough to tell him.

"No," he said quietly as they grew closer to the others. "No, I won't let you—"

"You don't get to decide whom I speak to or whose attentions I accept," Peggy muttered, plastering a smile across her face. "You lost that right, Ashcott."

"But I—"

"Ah, there you are," said Lord Castor smoothly, offering his arm to Peggy. "I was beginning to think I would have to send out a search party."

Peggy chuckled lightly as Luke came to a rather unsteady halt. "Oh, no, we were just looking at the herb garden. Are you going inside, Castor?"

"I shall go wherever you command me, my lady," said the blackguard.

Luke stared, unable to move, as the two of them walked arm and arm back into the Sedleys' home.

Just a few minutes ago, he had been kissing Peggy furiously—and she had responded, he knew she had. There was no possibility he had dreamed the way she parted her lips, or clung to his neck.

And now she was walking arm in arm with another man, pretending nothing had happened.

Luke cleared his throat and pulled his jacket down by the hem. Well, two could play at that game. He would be calm, and—

"My God, Ashcott, you look flushed," said Sedley conversationally, striding up to him in his riding gear. "You look like you could do with a cold bath!"

Luke sighed. "Several."

CHAPTER EIGHT

22 August, 1811

"AND THEN SHE said—"

"I don't think anyone wants to hear this story, my dear," the Duchess of Sedley said gently.

Peggy repressed a smile as she watched the Duke of Sedley wilt slightly under his wife's kind words, then rally almost immediately.

"Well, they are my guests. They will simply have to listen to whatever I say!"

Friendly laughter rippled through the drawing room.

Peggy sighed, allowing a smile to surface as she watched their host and hostess tease each other lightly, their affection quite obvious.

It was strange. When she was at home with Henry and Minny, it was easy to start to feel enclosed by their affection. It poured through everything they did, said, and even thought. It could be cloying, and Peggy had found herself desperate at times to get away. Perhaps that was only because it was her brother, though.

Seeing the Duke and Duchess of Sedley look at each other like that, as though they had never seen a more beautiful or more charming person in the world . . . well, it was painful. *Not painful,* Peggy attempted to correct her own thoughts. It just reminded her of what could have been. What should have been, if it hadn't been for Ashcott's stubbornness.

She carefully ensured she did not look up from the embroidery in her hands. He had taken the armchair directly opposite her position on the sofa. On purpose, she knew.

Well, Peggy was not going to give into the temptation of looking at him. She had already done a far more foolish thing this house party and given into the temptation of kissing him. Peggy hoped the evidence of that memory would not blossom up her neck to her cheeks. The last thing she needed was—

"You look a little warm, Lady Margaret."

She smiled wearily.

Lord Castor. The last three days had proven to her exactly what she did and did not want in a suitor. Unfortunately for the well-meaning viscount, it had become clear very quickly that he did not offer what Peggy wanted.

Still, it was not the man's fault. She supposed he meant well. But his tiresome flattery, inability to leave her be for more than an hour, and irritating way of constantly commenting on how she was looking—warm, hot, cold, tired—it was enough to drive a woman to distraction!

Thankfully, she would only have to endure his company for the duration of the house party. He was not part of her brother's set, so she would not have to suffer his presence again. Unless he did the unthinkable, and turned up at their home in London . . .

"I am a little warm, I suppose," Peggy said aloud, feeling the comment warranted at least a polite response. "The heat of the day."

"Oh, it has been something terrible, this weather!" said Mrs. Marnion, much to Peggy's relief. "Why, I was writing to my sister in Brighton, and she says—"

"Brighton? Tell me," said Miss Yates eagerly. "Has she been sea bathing? Is it truly as reviving as they say it is?"

"My sister, sea bathing! I should think not!" Mrs. Marnion looked genuinely affronted, much to Peggy's amusement. "I do not think that any lady of repute—"

"I have heard tell that the Duchess of Axwick considers a visit to Brighton incomplete unless she has taken a sea bath," said Peggy conversationally, not looking up from her embroidery as she spoke.

There was silence in the drawing room. The temptation to laugh was growing, but Peggy managed to control it.

She did, however, look up—momentarily forgetting who was seated opposite her.

There was a far too perceptive smile on Ashcott's face which she did not like at all. How dare he see her mischief for what it was!

"The *Duchess* of Axwick?" said Mrs. Marnion faintly. "Really?"

Peggy permitted the conversation to wash over her as Miss Yates replied. There was no more she could add to it, in any event. Henry had always been set against sea bathing, though precisely why she could not tell, so they had never gone to Brighton. She'd heard the Pavilion there was growing apace. Perhaps when it was completed, she would be able to prevail upon Henry to take her.

A small smile crept across her lips. Perhaps she would recruit Minny to assist her. It truly was astonishing. Henry had always been an excellent brother, but a resolute one. His wife, however, appeared able to bend him to her will without any apparent effort. Was that what it was like, being wedded to a person you adored?

She carefully did not look up again from her embroidery, despite the temptation to see whether Ashcott was still looking at her.

Adored. It was a strange word. One that had slipped through his lips not once, not twice, but several times.

A shiver tingled up Peggy's spine. She had believed it then. Believed it so wholeheartedly, she had thought his affection would never end, that it could outlast the world.

How wrong she had been.

"I suppose a mite of sea bathing would not do me a great injury," Mrs. Marnion was saying slowly.

"Unless you're swept out to sea, I suppose," said Lord Braedon jovially.

Peggy stifled another smile. Really, it was becoming a habit with this viscount. The man never seemed to know what to say!

"Is that likely?" asked a horrified Mrs. Marnion.

"Not in the slightest." The Duchess of Sedley's voice was calm and only hinted at the mirth she was probably feeling. "In fact, I have heard that there are specialized huts one can hire—"

"A hut? Me, in a hut?"

A clock chimed on the other side of the room. Ten o'clock.

Peggy placed her embroidering in her lap with relief. It was a perfectly suitable time for her to retire. No one would think ill of her or that she had tired of their company.

What had she been thinking, accepting an invitation from the Sedleys? Oh, they were fine enough people, she supposed, but dull. They had—likely as not—never done anything exciting. Not that Peggy recommended some of the excitement she and Luke had managed to find themselves in. Why, when they had snuck out of Almack's—

She pushed the thought aside swiftly as she rose to her feet. The less she thought about those days, the better. They were behind her.

"Oh, you're not retiring to bed, are you, Lady Margaret?" said the Duchess of Sedley hurriedly. "I thought we could play a game of charades, and you know how much I depend on your wit in these matters. Teams, everyone?"

Peggy's shoulders slumped as the room echoed with agreement to their hostess's suggestion.

Charades. She should have known she would not be permitted to slope off upstairs, where she could lose herself in a good book and the best company: her own.

"Two teams, I think," the Duke of Sedley was saying. "Men against women? Shall we wake old man Marnion from his nap?"

"That's hardly fair, there are already five men against us four," Miss Yates pointed out.

"I have no wish to play," said the young Mr. Marnion, face reddening. "I-I don't think—"

"Never fear, old man, it's not a school test," said Lord Braedon jovially. "Even if you're a dullard, you might do well here!"

There was a strained sort of silence after the viscount's words, but Peggy could not help but smile. There was not a malicious bone in the man's body, as far as she could see. Just a propensity to speak utter rubbish.

Ashcott cleared his throat. "In that case, young Marnion, you may be our adjudicator."

It was well done. Even Peggy, furious at the fact she had not thought of the solution herself, could not help but admit it, though she did so in the privacy of her own mind. She was hardly going to admit it aloud.

There was a great deal of hubbub for a few minutes, while the two teams separated out and seats were exchanged. Somehow, and Peggy was not entirely sure how, Lord Castor managed to find a seat beside her on the sofa.

"I suppose I shall have to support my team faithfully and play against you," he said with a grin.

Peggy attempted a smile. She really should not have encouraged him. She could not even call it flirting. Her brother would, but she wouldn't.

Whatever it was, she should not have done it so well with the viscount. He evidently thought her far more interested in him than she ever had been.

Ah, well. Just over a week, and it would all be over.

"Here's your first charade," said the young Mr. Marnion, who looked far happier now he was assured of not having to act out or guess at any of the charades.

A slip of paper was given to the Duchess of Sedley, who immediately grimaced.

"Oh, oh, oh—"

"That's not the charade, Mrs. Marnion," said the duchess swiftly.

Peggy tried to pay attention, she really did. The trouble was, charades had never truly interested her as a game to play with her family, and she wasn't particularly good at it, no matter what any hostess said.

In fact, it took almost ten minutes for the ladies to correctly guess the Duchess of Sedley's gesticulated offering, and the first word of the phrase was easy.

"Love?" Peggy guessed as the duchess clutched at her chest.

"Bravo!" said young Mr. Marnion, evidently losing himself in the excitement. "I-I mean, brava!"

The third word was just as simple. The Duchess of Sedley shaded her eyes as she peered in all directions, a worried look on her eyes.

"Sailor!" cried Mrs. Marnion.

"Lost," suggested Miss Yates.

"Brava!"

If they weren't careful, Peggy thought with a smile, *they would have to invite young Mr. Marnion onto their team.*

It was there that they got stuck. They knew the phrase was three words, but whatever it was the Duchess of Sedley was doing to approximate the middle word was utterly lost on them all.

And then it slipped into her mind. *Of course.*

"Love's Labor's Lost," Peggy said quietly.

The cheers of the ladies echoed around the drawing room, as the gentlemen protested that they had guessed the phrase long before any of them.

"Well done, Lady Margaret," said Lord Castor enthusiastically, touching her briefly on the arm.

It was just a brief touch. In many ways, Peggy hardly noticed it. In fact, in every way. If she had not been looking round at that precise moment, she would not have known he'd done it. There was no spark. No shiver up her arm, no tender longing that he touch her again, no wish that the moment could have elongated until they leaned together and their mouths drifted toward each other.

Well, there it was, Peggy thought sagely as the duchess took her seat and young Mr. Marnion turned to the gentleman to choose the next participant. If there had been any hope in Lord Castor securing her affections, surely that would have indicated it?

"Your Grace," the young Mr. Marnion was saying. "Here is your phrase."

Peggy turned to see what the Duke of Sedley would do—and her mouth fell open as Ashcott, scowling, took the slip of paper and rose to his feet.

This was the very last thing that she needed. She had sought excuses not to look at the blasted man—and now she was expected to! It was most unfair, and Peggy tried to look at the man's boots rather than his face, but the temptation to see how he was acting out whatever phrase it was ended up being too much.

He started off poorly.

"You can't do that!" protested Mrs. Marnion, as the duke clutched his chest just as the Duchess of Sedley had. "That's copying!"

"Is copying allowed, if it's the same word?" asked Ashcott.

Peggy rolled her eyes as scandalized groans filled the room.

"You can't say—"

"You've basically said the word!"

"How was I supposed to know that wasn't allowed?" protested Ashcott with a roguish grin.

Peggy scowled. It was most unfair that the man could look so handsome while being so infuriating. *And cheating!*

Besides, she knew now what his phrase was. It did not take a genius to work it out, and with the young Mr. Marnion in charge, she was sure she was right.

And that was why, just as Ashcott took a deep breath in preparation for his second word, the answer slipped from her lips before she could stop it.

"Love's Labor's Won."

Cheers went up from the ladies to her right, while groans rose again from the gentlemen.

"Erm," said the young Mr. Marnion awkwardly. "I-I don't think you're supposed to guess, Lady Margaret—"

"How could she not? The brain that woman has on her—I tell everyone I meet," the Duchess of Sedley began.

"Well done, Lady Margaret," said Ashcott in a low voice, his gaze sharp on hers.

Peggy swallowed.

Did he have to make it so obvious, the previous connection between them? It felt as though he were spelling it out to the entire room, making it impossible for them not to know.

The last thing she wanted was to think about it. What their life could have been. What fate could have had in store for them, if he had not been so much of a coward to run from it.

Something painful stirred. *This could have been their house party.*

Not here, obviously. At whatever manor Ashcott had in the country. They could have chosen their guests, their food, the activities. They would have laughed with their friends. Perhaps he and Henry would be close by now.

And she would have been happy.

Peggy tried to push away the thought. What good would it do her? She could not retrieve that life—it was gone. Lost to her months ago.

And every time he looked at her like that, as though the whole world revolved around her, someone would make a sarcastic remark. Someone would comment, perhaps, about the supposed engagement that had managed to leak to the gossips of the *ton* last year.

"I never truly understood those plays," said the Duke of Sedley happily.

Peggy breathed a sigh of relief as the conversation wandered away from the game of charades and toward the Shakespeare plays themselves.

"Losing love," sighed Miss Yates. "It sounds like a terrible fate."

"If a man is foolish enough to lose someone's affections then that is his mistake, his burden to bear," said a bitter voice.

For a moment, Peggy looked around to see who had spoken. It was certainly someone who had known real pain. Someone who was not ready to think about the next part of their life. She pitied them.

Then she saw that every face in the drawing room was looking at her. Only then did she realize.

Oh, goodness. It wasn't she who had spoken, was it?

"That's a very harsh view, Lady Margaret," said Lord Braedon with uncharacteristic seriousness. "You don't think second chances—"

"I think second chances are for those who are ready to be hurt again," Peggy said awkwardly. *How on earth could she change the topic of conversation?*

"I quite agree," said Miss Yates quietly.

Their eyes met, and Peggy could not help but wonder. She knew so little about Miss Yates. Was it possible—

"And you don't think," came a gruff voice, "there is any circumstance in which a man could be forgiven? That he could, in time, come to learn from his mistake and wish to rectify the situation?"

Peggy's heart stopped.

Then it started again. *It was a momentary aberration,* she tried to tell herself. Complete coincidence that it occurred just when her eyes met Ashcott's.

Met the eyes of a man who she would have given everything to, if she could. Who had offered her nothing when she had offered everything. She could see that now, with the beauty of hindsight. She had been willing to give Luke Beauchamp, Duke of Ashcott, anything.

And he had walked away.

Thankfully the rest of the room's conversation had drifted back to the charades, whether they should just give up on teams and allow anyone to guess.

So no one watched as Peggy held Ashcott's gaze and refused to look away.

It was not over.

Oh, despite everything she had told the man in Bath, she could not pretend there weren't still feelings there. She had loved him too dearly for him to entirely lose his hold on her. But Peggy had not realized until she had arrived at the Sedleys' just how deep those passions were.

Because a part of her wanted to say yes. *Yes, apologize. Properly. Tell me why you did it, and how much you regret it, and how sorry you are that I was hurt. Kiss me. Kiss away all the regrets we surely share, and then we can be together.*

But he hadn't, had he? And Peggy had given him a chance. She had allowed him to speak utter nonsense in the library, and he'd said nothing of meaning. Nothing of his affections.

No matter how desperately she wanted Ashcott to be redeemed in her eyes, only he could do that. And he hadn't done it.

Peggy straightened her back stiffly and glared back at Ashcott. "Forgiveness? Redemption? No circumstances whatsoever."

Her soul rebelled against the sentiment, clamoring to be heard, but Peggy wouldn't listen. She had already been too hurt before. She deserved the very best in life, she knew, and the Duke of Ashcott simply wasn't the best. Pain wasn't best.

"Peggy," he said in a low voice.

Perhaps if they had been alone, she would have rushed to his arms. There was such feeling in Ashcott's voice, such depths she had never heard before.

Peggy gasped. It was impossible not to. She had never seen

such—such vulnerability in Ashcott's eyes. Just for an instant, a flicker, a moment, she had seen more hurt in his face than she had known could exist.

Did he feel it too? Was he as lost as she was?

"Lady Margaret, what do you think?"

"Wh-What?" Peggy stammered, turning to her left.

Lord Castor was smiling, as though they had been sharing a private joke.

What on earth was he talking about? What did she think about what?

"I-I beg your pardon?" she tried again, hoping he had not noticed her rudeness.

"We were discussing, Lord Braedon and I, whether or not it would be best to play charades as a group," Lord Castor said with what he evidently thought was a winning smile. "I think any team that does not have you on it is greatly disadvantaged, after all."

Peggy stared blankly. *Charades? Teams? What did any of that matter? Ashcott was about to—*

Her gaze flickered back to the armchair where Ashcott had been sitting. It was empty.

CHAPTER NINE

23 August, 1811

"THE BRACING OUTDOORS!" declared Luke. "That's what I need. All I need."

He wasn't entirely sure who he was trying to convince, himself or the Duke of Sedley who was giving him a rather shrewd look.

"Bracing outdoors," Sedley repeated. "In August."

It was a daft thing to say, now Luke thought about it—but he needed an excuse for this early ride, and only something daft would convince his host.

Though every moment he spent with the Duke of Sedley, the more he realized the man was hardly a dolt. In fact, Luke would hazard to say that he was one of the cleverest men he knew. He was so clever, in fact, that Sedley seemed to go out of his way to ensure no one knew just how clever he was.

Interesting.

Luke did not reply but instead tightened the saddle on the steed he was borrowing from his host. The early hour did not prevent the heat of the day from already curling around his collar and underneath his riding habit. And they would have to be back within the hour to avoid boiling themselves or their animals. But that was of no matter. All he needed to do was get out of the house. Get away from Peggy, and her flirting, and—

"Damn," Luke muttered.

His inattention had caused part of the buckle to suddenly wrench open. The prong raked across his skin, leaving a trail of red, beaded blood.

"You all right, man?"

"Never better," Luke replied to his host's question.

He put his thumb in his mouth to staunch the bleeding. Well, this was the last thing he needed—but at least the day could not get any worse.

"Sucking your thumb, Ashcott? A bit old for that, aren't you?" asked Lord Castor jovially as he stepped into the stable.

Luke dropped his hand to his side and glowered at the interloper, before remembering he had no personal monopoly on riding. Unfortunately.

"Castor," he said darkly, before turning to his horse and mounting without a block.

"Ah, Castor! I'm glad you got my note—I don't think old Marnion is up to a ride this morning, not after the amount of port I saw the man drink," said Sedley in a cheerful voice. "And young Marnion . . . well . . ."

"If that man is able to stand after that cigar he decided was his favorite, I shall be astonished," said Castor with a laugh. "Shall we?"

Of course, Luke thought as the three men rode out of the stable and toward the trail toward the forest. All he'd wanted was a quiet beginning to the morning. A chance to gather his thoughts. Not think about Peggy. Ask Sedley subtly if he had ever been to France. Not think about Peggy. Stay cool for as long as possible. Not think about Peggy.

And now he had to have his lordship with them.

God, it was infuriating!

"I must thank you, Your Grace, for inviting me for this house party," the idiot was saying sycophantically. "I had never expected such affection in your note, and I must say . . ."

Luke stopped listening to him.

It was easy enough. You spend enough time in France, you swiftly learn what to hear and what not to hear. How to focus on one particular conversation in a room, ignoring all others.

And so he listened to the forest instead of the banal conversation to his left. The movement of deer deep in the trees. The birds. The way rustling suggested at boar, or perhaps an overly large pheasant.

But try as he might, it was impossible for Luke to entirely ignore the conversation. Particularly when it mentioned—

"—Lady Margaret," said Castor with a grin Luke did not like. "Good God, I've never seen a woman like her!"

"Have a care, Castor," said Sedley easily. "She's without her brother here."

"Oh, I wouldn't consider—"

"What would you consider, Castor?" Luke found himself asking.

The two other men stared curiously, and Luke did everything he could to keep his face impassive.

It was not an entirely unfair questions. Probably. After all, he hadn't directly come out and said what he wished.

"What are your intentions toward Lady Margaret Everleigh?"

The words tingled on Luke's tongue but he managed to keep them behind his teeth. He was not father, nor brother, nor friend of any description to have the right to ask that question.

The trouble was, it was clear Lord Castor understood what he truly meant. A knowing smile flickered across his face, and when he spoke, it was with a nonchalance Luke knew only came when carefully considered.

"And what is it to you, pray? What is she to you?"

The Duke of Sedley was riding between them and could evidently sense something was amiss. "Now, gentlemen—"

"It is as Sedley says. The Lady Margaret is alone here," Luke said, hating he had to be so formal when speaking about the woman he—

Well. *Loved.*

Why was it so difficult to think? Impossible to say, yes, but surely in the privacy of his own mind, he should be bold enough to think it?

"Well, I am seeing to it that she does not feel alone," said Castor. His smile remained, but the friendliness had gone from his eyes. "Not that it's anything to do with you, Ashcott."

Luke ignored the rudeness. It was easy to do, when dealing with a man like Castor.

His predatory tone, however . . .

"Do not get comfortable," Luke said, knowing with every syllable that he should hold his tongue, and simultaneously knowing he could not. "Lady Margaret does not like—"

"And who are you to say what or who she does not like?" Castor shot back. "Save for the fact that she clearly does not appreciate your company, Ashcott."

The last word was spoken like an insult.

In a way, Luke supposed it was. His reputation had never been particularly brilliant. A rake, a scoundrel, someone who acted first and did not bother to apologize.

It was why, in part, he thought Peggy had been rather intrigued by him. The chance to be around a rake, she had once said to him, was well worth the additional scandal. Neither of them had planned on falling in love.

"Hold fire there, chaps," said Sedley uneasily. "I am sure—"

"I think I will turn back," Luke said coldly. *One more minute spent in that gollumpus's company, and he may just say something he would regret.* Even more than what he had already said. "I'll see you back at the house. Good day, Sedley."

Ignoring completely the other gentleman, Luke turned his borrowed steed around and encouraged him to canter back along the trail.

Old Castor would think he had given up. It was irritating beyond belief, but Luke knew he could not stand the man's presence any further. Every moment spent with him was merely another reminder that it was his attentions, and not Luke's, being welcomed by the one woman who truly mattered.

And it was because his thoughts wended that way that Luke at first did not believe his eyes. He was thinking too much about Peggy. That must explain why he could see her approaching him along the path that encircled the lawn on a steed of her own.

Luke blinked. The mirage, if mirage it was, remained.

As the two horses grew closer, he slowed his down to a trot, hardly wishing to miss a moment of this opportunity to look at Peggy—a very real Peggy—without anyone else around.

Oh, she was beautiful. The way she sat on a horse, it was as though they were one. She was a lady, which meant that she had been half raised on horses—but even so, there were few others in the *ton* who had her way with a steed.

Luke's stomach lurched. The way she moved so fluidly . . . well, it caused a gentleman to think of things different than riding. Riding a horse, at any rate.

It was with no expectation that she would mirror him that Luke pulled on his horse's reins and slowed the beast to a complete stop. Just to watch her pass by without any need to hide his appreciation for her form. That was all he hoped for.

It was rather startling, therefore, when Peggy slowed her horse to stand alongside his.

Her cheeks were pink. "Have I missed it?"

Luke blinked. "Missed what?"

Why couldn't he string more than two words together coherently when he was around her? He was supposed to be one of the wittiest men in Society! Yet here he was, sounding like a perfect fool.

He cleared his throat and began again. "If I can be of any assistance to you—"

"Oh, save that for Miss Yates," Peggy shot back, tossing her head back as the sunshine rippled across her riding habit. "The ride this morning. Lord Castor—"

She said more words, Luke was sure, but the boiling anger in his bones made hearing anything impossible.

When her mouth stopped moving, he said stiffly, "You have missed the beginning. Castor and Sedley are farther along the trail."

"Oh. Good," said Peggy.

And yet she did not move. She just sat on her horse, allowing it to munch happily at the grass on the verge.

Looking at him.

Luke swallowed. He could hardly recall the last time Peggy had looked at him. Really looked at him. Without ire, without irritation. Without saying something cutting then marching away, leaving him to collect up the pieces of his life once again and try to put them back together.

What was he supposed to do now? Had she not made perfectly clear last night at the charades, as she and Lord Castor had whispered together, that she had chosen the man who would have the honor of being her husband?

"You . . . you're going on a ride, then," Luke said helplessly.

He always felt helpless in her company—yet strangely, Peggy did not immediately quip about his foolish remark.

Instead, and most unaccountably, she flushed. "Y-Yes. At least, I thought I was not too far behind."

"You're not," said Luke woodenly. "They're only a bit farther along."

"Oh. That's good."

"Yes. Very good."

What are you doing, a voice inside Luke's head screamed. *Can't you tell she wants to talk to you? Why else would she be allowing her horse to stand here right beside yours?*

Say something meaningful, you dolt!

"I . . . uh . . ."

If only he hadn't been so foolish as to ask her that direct question yesterday evening. He couldn't have made it more obvious his heart was just waiting to be broken by her.

"And you don't think there is any circumstance in which a man could be forgiven? That he could, in time, come to learn from his mistake and wish to rectify the situation?"

Peggy had had the chance, hadn't she, to restore a little hope in his life? To make it clear that what they had could perhaps, one day, be found again.

She had taken that chance and trodden it underfoot.

"Forgiveness? Redemption? No circumstances whatsoever."

Luke swallowed. *This was mere politeness*, he tried to tell himself. Anyone would pause for a moment and speak with someone they met on a path. It was nothing more than that.

Yet something had changed between them. Despite her direct words last night, the Peggy of yesterday would not have halted her horse to speak to him at all, let alone lingered.

What was going on?

"You're going back." Peggy was staring—and when he caught her eye, she looked at her reins as though she hadn't been examining him at all.

"Y-Yes," he said. Clearing his throat, he said in a far more certain voice, "Yes, I didn't appreciate the company as much as I thought I would."

A flicker of concern across Peggy's face—a concern Luke did not understand, until she said quietly, "I thought you liked the Duke of Sedley."

Relief rushed through his bones. *Yes, this was a safe topic.* The Sedleys were good people and most excellent hosts. Talking of them would be absolutely fine.

"Oh, I like Sedley well enough," Luke said easily, his tongue loosening after the tension faded. "No, it was Castor that was the . . . I mean . . . oh, blast."

And just like that, he had managed to entirely unravel himself again.

Luke shuffled uncomfortably on his horse. The saddle wasn't entirely to his liking, but worst of all, neither was the look Peggy was giving him. Her previous look hadn't been exactly sincere—

but it had been downright welcoming compared to the way she was looking at him now.

"Castor?"

"I don't want you talking to him any more than you can help it," Luke said, throwing all caution to the wind. *Oh, he was in it up to his neck now, wasn't he? Might was well keep going.* "He's not the sort of chap—"

"What do you know about the right sort of chap?" Peggy asked with a raised eyebrow.

Luke hesitated.

Because I've seen the absolute worst of men at the Dulverton Club, the one your precious brother thinks is so wonderful, he wanted to say.

I've seen the lies, and treachery, and desperation of France.

I've seen what good men look like. And Castor isn't one of them.

"Let's just say," he attempted to say magnanimously, "I do not think Castor a good fit for you."

It was the wrong thing to say. With that excellent horsewomanship Luke knew so well, Peggy nudged her steed closer, as though the words she was about to say were crucially important.

Luke tried not to luxuriate in Peggy's closeness. She was not doing it for that reason. No matter how much he may wish to convince himself, Peggy had been perfectly clear. She did not wish a return of his affections.

Still. A man couldn't be blamed for—

"You may have misunderstood me," Peggy said softly, looking up into Luke's face.

His loins jolted and his manhood twitched. *Now this was more like it.* Peggy, speaking to him in a low voice, as though to a friend. As though to someone who was more.

A Peggy, moreover, who was a mere foot away. Why, that was nothing to two people nimble on a horse. All they would have to do is lean across and—

"I told you I didn't need you to tell me what to do, or not do, about Lord Castor," said Peggy quietly, refusing to look away. "And I meant it."

Frustration poured through Luke, and once again he spoke rashly. "Peggy—"

"Lady Margaret!"

"Fine!" Luke exploded, pushed beyond all endurance. "I'll call you whatever you want, my lady, but it doesn't change what happened between us!"

"That is in the past," Peggy said, though the high color in her cheeks suggested otherwise. "You cannot—you have no right to tell me what to do!"

"No right?" Luke growled.

All his possessiveness, his absolute certainty until a few days ago that Peggy would swiftly come to realize just how much she still cared for him, his determination to have her—it was all rising to the surface.

Uncontrolled. Demanding. Insistent.

It was a good thing they were atop different horses, Luke thought angrily. If they were standing on the path, it would not be long before she was pushed up against that fence post and shown, not told, that she was his.

His gaze flickered to her lips. When it returned to her eyes, it was to see Peggy looking at his mouth.

Desire burned through him. *Why did she have to deny herself the very thing they both knew she wanted?*

"I want to kiss you," Luke breathed.

He had not meant to. His approach of never telling anyone what he was truly thinking was melting away in the face of the ferocious passion sizzling between them.

Between both of them—wasn't it?

"Well, you can't," Peggy murmured, though her breathing had quickened. "You know how that will end."

"With you calling out my name," Luke said in a low voice. *Dear God, she was enough to tempt the very devil himself.* "With you on your back on that grass and—"

"And then what?" She did not seem to be able to stop herself speaking.

He gloried in the way Peggy continued to lean, closer and closer, until there were just inches between them. Their horses were touching. Surely it could not be long before they too—

"And then I will make you cry out again, but this time not with my name," Luke said, words stumbling off his tongue as the image of what he was describing filled his vision. "Because you won't be able to think of words. You'll be so lost in the pleasure I give you—"

"Luke," Peggy whispered, eyelashes fluttering. "You . . . you can't say such things—"

"Why not?" Luke said aggressively, reaching out for her. "Peggy, I—"

And somehow that broke the moment. The instant he said her name, it was over. The pliant, desirous Peggy disappeared, leaving only the fiery Peggy behind.

She swiftly moved her horse from him. "Never speak to me like that ag—"

"You liked it," said Luke, excitement tingling up his temples.

Peggy didn't try to deny it. He could see the truth in her cheeks, the heaviness of her breathing, the way she appeared so disconcerted.

Dear God, she liked it. She liked him—she wanted him, even if she would not admit it. Not even to herself.

"You may be a duke," Peggy began.

"Your duke," said Luke with a lopsided grin.

Happiness was filling his lungs, every breath increasing the pressure in his chest. It was all going to be all right. Somehow, he didn't know how—but he would reach her. The Peggy that was inside, the true Peggy.

The Peggy right now was looking at him, scandalized. "You are not my—you may be a duke, but that doesn't make you perfect, or able to control me, or—or likely to have me!"

Her hands tightened on the reins.

"You want me," said Luke confidently, leaning back and trying to catch his own breath. "And it's only a matter of time before you realize that, Peg."

The glare she subjected him to was marvelous to behold.

He grinned. "Dear God. How have I managed to live without you?"

Peggy snorted. "Quite easily, as it seems. Why, you—"

"There you are! I am sorry, Lady Margaret, I presumed you had decided against such an early ride!"

Luke whirled around.

There, behind them on the path, were Lord Castor and the Duke of Sedley. Castor looked pink. Sedley looked mortified.

"Lord Castor!"

Luke heard the embarrassment in Peggy's voice and winced.

So, just how much had they heard? How much had they seen? Was Peggy's reputation entirely ruined, or was just a hint of it stained?

"We've just come around the corner," said Sedley, with a perceptive look in Luke's direction. "What a fine chance that we should meet you here."

Luke swallowed. *Thank God for honorable men.* "Yes. Yes indeed. How fortunate."

CHAPTER TEN

24 August, 1811

"—AND THEN I saw immediately what he was trying to do! The clever old thing thought I wouldn't notice the absolute pin trick, but I spotted it the moment I saw his bishop was right there. Well, I thought to myself, there's only one way to get me out of this nonsense . . ."

Peggy nodded. Then shook her head, just in case that was a better response.

It would have been easier to know if she'd been paying attention to Viscount Castor's words, of course, but for some reason, she just couldn't.

Not some reason, Peggy thought with a wry smile. *One particular reason. One particular person.*

But Ashcott wasn't in the morning room. Claiming he had some business to complete, and after being offered the use of the Sedleys' study to complete it, the Duke of Ashcott had disappeared after breakfast.

And she, Peggy told herself firmly, *did not mind.*

Of course she didn't. What care she where Luke was?

Where the Duke of Ashcott was, she corrected silently as Castor continued to waffle on about this chess match in which he had performed so well.

"—not enough pieces on the board, I thought. After all, it was going to be remarkably difficult for anyone to secure a win with only six pieces, and one of them a pawn! But then I said to myself . . ."

Peggy nodded again.

They were not alone in the morning room. Now that would have been scandalous. Miss Yates was reading a book whose title she could not quite make out from this distance, and the Duchess of Sedley was going over a few things with her housekeeper, a stern looking woman who melted in the presence of her mistress.

"The fish course?"

"Do we have any trout?"

"I believe the gentlemen will be fishing this afternoon, Your Grace—"

"Well, we can't depend on them. You've seen Sedley with a rod. No, I think it best if you purchase some from the village."

Peggy settled herself deeper in her chair.

It wasn't precisely the fascinating conversation she had hoped for, but it wasn't too dull. Mrs. Marnion had given up hinting she was the perfect match for the younger Mr. Marnion, at least. That had been excruciating.

And it wasn't too stifling in here yet. At merely half past ten in the morning, Peggy knew it would soon heat up, but as there was nothing she could do about it, and Lord Castor was being so obliging as to provide a natural wash of sound around her.

"—few people would have thought of that. I pride myself, naturally, in keeping my skills sharp. It can be difficult if you cannot find an opponent who is suitably challenging. I like to ask people, when they attend the Dulverton . . ."

Peggy smiled to herself as her breathing slowed, a sleepy sensation creeping around her eyes. She'd never grow accustomed to hearing that. Their grandfather had been most insistent that the club he'd founded be named after them, and as he was putting up most of the money, no one seemed willing to argue.

Though it was still odd to hear in conversation.

"—not boring you, am I, Lady Margaret?"

"Not in the slightest," Peggy said cordially—though not too cordially. One did not wish to create ideas.

Lord Castor beamed. "It is such a pleasure to talk chess!"

It was on the tip of her tongue to point out that as she had hardly said six words together, she was not sure this conversation could be described as, in fact, a conversation.

But what was the point? In a matter of days she wouldn't be seeing the man again, except perhaps at Almack's when she would be unable to avoid the connection. Beyond that, Lord Castor would become one of a number of gentlemen Peggy had met, liked enough to tolerate but no more, and rarely seen again.

And for the moment he was a useful distraction when she needed to avoid a certain gentleman's gaze.

"I don't want you talking to him any more than you can help it."

A flicker of stubbornness soared through her. If Luke didn't want her going anywhere near Lord Castor, then that was precisely what she was going to do. Who did he think he was, ordering her about? Even her brother knew better than to attempt something so ridiculous.

"Lady Margaret?"

"—chess is a far more difficult game than most people realize. In truth, I think the word 'game' is unfairly simple for—"

"I say, Lady Margaret?"

Peggy blinked. The housekeeper had ceased speaking to the Duchess of Sedley and was now standing before her with a letter in her hand.

"Y-Yes?" she said, struggling to sit upright.

Goodness. The atmosphere of the room and the boredom of Lord Castor's company had put her into a far deeper stupor than she had imagined.

"I am sorry to disturb you, Lady Margaret, and you, Lord Castor," said the housekeeper with a look Peggy did not appreciate. "But there is a letter for you."

"For me?" Peggy said blankly, takin the letter as it was handed to her.

A letter? Goodness, who could be writing to her?

For a moment, just a moment, excitement crackled through her bones. Surely Luke would not be so scandalous as to write to her, would he? It was most indecorous for a gentleman to be in correspondence with a lady at the best of times, but while they were both guests under the same roof . . .

The scandalous nature of her guess, far from annoying her, sent a frisson of joy through Peggy—joy she swiftly attempted, and failed, to stifle.

What could Luke possibly write that he could not say face to face? That was what she had expected, wasn't it? That he was here to make some sort of big declaration.

Well, she'd soon put a stop to that, Peggy thought shortly as she turned the letter over and over in her hands. He'd had his chance. He'd said nothing. And he could not expect her to wait around and just wait for him to—

"Lady Margaret?"

Peggy focused. The housekeeper had gone, but Lord Castor was still beside her.

"Are you not going to open your letter?" he said with a smile. "I shall leave you to it, of course, if it is an admirer seeking your hand."

Try as she might, Peggy could not quite laugh naturally. "What an idea!"

What an idea indeed. The thought had settled, digging into her hopes and making her wonder . . .

But the moment she actually looked down at the direction, written in a bold yet untidy hand, her heart sank.

Not that she had been hoping it was from Luke, Peggy tried to tell herself.

"It's from my brother, not an admirer," she said aloud.

"Well for that, I shall be thankful," said Lord Castor with— was that a wink? Surely not! "In any case, I will leave you to your reading. Until we meet again, Lady Margaret."

Peggy did her best not to roll her eyes as he bowed and left the morning room. Until they met again? They were guests at the same house party! She could barely move in this place for tripping over him, he was so carefully keeping to her heels. Honestly!

Still, the letter was a pleasant excuse not to have to sit and listen to him witter on about chess any longer.

The Dulverton seal was swiftly broken. Peggy leaned back in her chair in the gentle silence of the morning room to see what was so important that Henry could not wait a week until she was home.

Peg,

Well, you've done it! You've abandoned me. I hope your days have been filled with laughter and games, more food than is good for you, and that you've met a few ladies who can become your friends.

It's not good for you to spend so much time alone, you know. I've always said it, and now Minny is saying it too, which means I must have been right all along.

Little Henry sends his love, as much as he can. You know, I honestly think he laughed at something I said the other day! I told Minny, and she said that it was entirely possible. Then she said almost everything I said was laughable, which quite put me in my place.

I know it was difficult, deciding to leave town and to spend time with the Sedleys whom you barely like. But I honestly think it was the right decision. Getting out of Bath away from that man—I will not even write his name, I loathe the brute too well—was absolutely the right decision.

You may have made mistakes in that direction in the past. I will not speak of it, and instead merely note I am glad I returned when I did and I am proud of you, more than I can say, for refusing his advances since.

Hopefully it will not be too long before I can see you settled and married to a man who truly deserves you. The best thing in life is love. Find it, if you can.

Your tiresome brother,
Henry

PS. I heard tell from Wincham, of all people, that there is a certain Viscount Castor at the Sedleys' with you. Apparently he's a good sort, whatever that means.

PPS. Minny sends her love. Did I already say that?

PPPS. Write back and tell me about this Castor fellow. A potential match?

It was with great relief that Peggy read her brother's letter without the eager eye of Lord Castor over her shoulder. To think, he might have seen her brother's ridiculous suggestion that Lord Castor and she might be a match.

Peggy folded up the letter. Absolutely not.

Then she unfolded it.

Getting out of Bath, away from that man—I will not even write his name, I loathe the brute too well—was absolutely the right decision.

You may have made mistakes in that direction in the past. I will not speak of it, and instead merely note I am glad I returned when I did, and I am proud of you, more than I can say, for refusing his advances since.

Well, she had. Mostly.

Entirely, Peggy congratulated herself. Really, all she had done was try to convince Luke—convince the Duke of Ashcott to leave her alone. She could not have been more plain.

Except that moment when she had revealed just how deeply he had hurt her.

And that moment when he had kissed her, and it had been like coming home, and she had clung to him just for a moment before she realized what she was doing.

And that outrageous conversation when he had muttered just what he would like to do to her . . .

"And then I will make you cry out again, but this time not with my name. Because you won't be able to think of words. You'll be so lost in the pleasure I give you—"

Peggy swallowed and folded the letter back up again. *Other than that, she had done rather well.*

What woman could do better in the company of Luke Beauchamp, the Duke of Ashcott?

"The heat of the day can be quite tiresome, can't it?"

Peggy started. Miss Yates was looking over with a sympathetic look—so sympathetic, in fact, it was almost as though she had managed to read Henry's letter.

Which was preposterous. Of course she hadn't.

"Very tiresome," Peggy managed.

"I think the drawing room is cooler," said Miss Yates. "But it simply doesn't have the light I need to read."

"That is a marvelous idea," said Peggy, rising to her feet gratefully. "I think I will spend an hour in the drawing room, Miss Yates, Your Grace. Just to cool down."

Just to collect myself. Just to bring myself to my senses. Just to ensure that I am able to appear later in company without staring at Luke as though my life depended on him.

"Excellent idea, my dear," said the duchess vaguely. She was now reading a novel of her own and appeared entirely lost in it. "The gong will go for luncheon, you know how it does. On the lawn again."

Peggy curtseyed to them both and strode confidently out of the morning room.

But when she had gone along the corridor a little way, her confidence wavered and her footsteps halted. The Sedleys' country estate was not overly large, but she was still not entirely accustomed to the different corridors. One landscape painting looked much like another, and they'd decorated the place almost exactly the same along every route.

So was it left at the end of this corridor, or right, to find the drawing room?

Peggy hesitated, her brother's letter still clutched in her hands. Left. No, right. She was almost certain it was right.

She had only been walking along the corridor another few seconds, however, when she realized that she had gone the wrong direction. That vase looked completely different from the one outside the dining room, and that was beside the drawing room, wasn't it?

Turning on her heel, Peggy was quite ready to retrace her steps and find the drawing room until something made her pause.

A voice. And not just any voice. Luke's voice.

"—don't know what to do with myself—"

Peggy halted, heart thundering in her chest. It wasn't natural for it to go from calmly beating along to suddenly roaring like this! But she could do nothing about it. Luke had been speaking low, pain in his voice, a sense of sharing a confidence in his tone.

It was probably most uncouth of her. But Peggy did it anyway.

Creeping along the corridor, most grateful for the thick Axminster rug softening her footsteps, Peggy crept over to a door that was slightly ajar. That was where Luke's voice had seemed to come from. If she was very quiet—

"I must admit, I still don't fully understand," came another voice, low and urgent. "Explain it to me again."

That was the duke's voice—the Duke of Sedley, that was. *This must be his study,* Peggy thought with a thrill. The study from which Luke could write some letters to his steward.

But this manner of conversation did not sound like they were discussing matters of their estates. Oh, no. This sounded far more intoxicatingly secret.

Something she should most assuredly not be listening to.

Peggy did not move.

"It's all painfully and agonizingly simple," came Luke's voice, stronger now but just as despairing. "I first met Peggy—"

"Lady Margaret."

"Don't you start doing that, too," shot back Luke's irritated voice.

Peggy stifled a laugh. If she had known just how greatly it annoyed the man, she would have started doing it sooner.

"Margaret, then. She and I met at Almack's, and she was a pretty thing, and I thought—well, I was bored," came Luke's quiet voice.

The smile on her lips immediately faded.

Bored? He was bored? That memory had been one of the most precious of her life. Gazes meeting across a crowded room, a hurried introduction, talking all night to no one else because his conversation was so riveting.

And he had looked at her like . . . like . . .

Peggy drew herself up, determined to forget that the memory ever happened. *What a rake! What a charlatan! She should never even have considered forgiving him. In fact, she would barge in there and tell him—*

"I fell in love with her after about ten minutes," Luke's voice continued. "I couldn't think of anyone else, anything else. You know, we spent all evening talking."

"Talking?" The Duke of Sedley's voice sounded disbelieving.

Luke's laugh was more a bark. "Trust me, I wanted more—even a dance, the chance to touch her. But damn it man, I couldn't stop talking to her! The woman has the mind of a wit, a true wit, not one of these Society ninnies who parrot back the last joke they heard."

Peggy's mouth fell open.

He fell in love with her then? The very first time they met?

Now why on earth had Luke Beauchamp never mentioned that?

"I still don't understand," came the duke's calm voice. "You liked her. She liked you, which shows there's no accounting for tastes—"

"Steady on there—"

"So why have I never seen the two of you together until now?" persisted the Duke of Sedley's voice. "Why didn't you marry her, man?"

Peggy frowned. That was a very good question—a question she had never received a satisfactory answer to.

Until, it appeared, now.

"Because I am a damned stubborn fool." A heavy sigh that could only be Luke's crept through the gap between the door and its frame. "Because her brother—"

"Careful now," interrupted the duke's voice. "I'll not hear anything against Dulverton."

"Oh, I'm sure he's a terrific fellow," came Luke's sarcastic reply. "As long as you aren't discovered hiding behind a curtain in his drawing room, just after proposing matrimony to his sister, when you never even asked the man's permission to be courting her."

There was silence in the study. Peggy could feel every throb of her pulse, every sharp intake of breath. She was concentrating so hard, she almost thought she could hear the sunlight drifting down through the window onto the rug.

Then there was a heavy sigh inside the study. "Damn."

"My biggest regret," Luke's voice said, hollow and empty. "A regret I'll never escape. I'll spend the rest of my life, Sedley, knowing that I should be by that woman's side. And I'm forever barred from it. And blast it all, for good reason."

Confusion swirled through Peggy's mind, but it was swiftly overcome with something she had not expected to feel in Luke's presence.

Hope.

He had loved her. Truly loved her, and not for her position, or her wealth, or the little beauty she possessed. Because of her. Her conversation. Her wit, whatever that was. He regretted not marrying her. He had actually said it—Luke, with his mouth, said that he regretted not being with her.

Peggy could hardly stand. It was fortunate indeed that she

could lean against the wall, for else she would surely have fallen.

Luke loved her. He wanted her still, after all this time. Even after the sharp words she had shot in both his general and quite specific direction.

Confused feelings twisted in conflict in her mind, in her heart. Hope, yes. But also despair. Anger. Bitterness that he had not been able to say such words to her. Relief that she had discovered the truth, regardless.

They congealed into something akin to . . .

Peggy wasn't sure. What was she supposed to do now? How could she ever confront him with the truth—and did she want to? Was she ready to once more reveal herself to this man who had so unceremoniously walked away?

Was she willing to risk this all again?

"What are you going to do now?" the Duke of Sedley asked.

Peggy leaned closer to the gap in the door, hoping beyond hope they couldn't see her.

"Do? There's nothing to do," came Luke's defeated voice. "She's chosen Castor."

There was a loud snort from their host. "That dullard?"

"Perhaps that's what she wants," were Luke's quiet words. "Perhaps she's been too pained by her interactions with me, Society's rake. Perhaps . . . perhaps she's decided there's something better out there for her."

"What, boredom?"

"Safety," came Luke's heavy sigh. "The best thing in life, I think, is to love and be loved. But perhaps for Peggy, it's to know you can't be hurt again. And damn it, I wouldn't blame her."

Peggy swallowed.

He knew her so well. The thought had crossed her mind, not only with Lord Castor, but with a few other gentlemen she had been so unfortunate as to meet since Luke had left for France.

Yet she had never been able to reconcile herself to the idea of not being loved. Truly loved. For herself.

"Come now, we are supposed to be looking at these accounts," came Luke's voice. There was a sniff. "Not pouting."

"I'm not the one pouting," pointed out the Duke of Sedley's voice with a laugh. "Fine, fine. Let me just step into the library, there's a book I think would—"

Half skipping, half running down the corridor, Peggy quickly turned a corner and leaned against the wall, breathing heavily.

Well. What on earth was she supposed to do now?

CHAPTER ELEVEN

25 August, 1811

I T WAS A relief, after the heat of the day and his own frustrated passions, to walk outside in the cool night air.

Luke glanced at the moon. Almost full. The brilliant moonlight soared through the trees, scattering silver light across the gravel path crunching under his feet.

The peace of kitchen gardens was something he had always craved. When his father had tired of forcing him to hide his emotions, when his mother had finished berating him for being soft, this was where Luke had always come.

Well, not here. The kitchen gardens of the Sedleys were not as broad, nor were they surrounded by a red brick wall, as his childhood gardens had been.

But still. There were sufficient similarities to immediately calm Luke's frayed nerves. The scent of the onions and leeks. The remains of this year's rhubarb. The apple and pear trees in a small grove. The patch of potatoes, their beautiful flowers suggesting an impressive crop for the Sedley kitchens in the autumn. Luke breathed out a slow, steady sigh as he stopped before a bed of plants clearly designed for cut flowers. Mignonette, peonies now gone, pinks, sweet Williams.

There was something about kitchen gardens. The growth, the possibility. The potential for new life and new beginnings.

The tension around his shoulders started to melt away as the inexplicable scent of lemons rose in the air. If he could just remain here for a full hour, undisturbed, he knew he would feel more himself again. It must already be past eleven—the rest of the guests had retired to bed, including—

"Luke!"

Hardly able to believe his ears, Luke slowly turned around.

He almost staggered back. It was Peggy, and she looked like nothing more than a nymph. As though a goddess had decided to wander to the earth.

The white gown she had been wearing at dinner and later in the drawing room looked silver in the moonlight. Her dark curls were half pinned up, half falling past her shoulders. She had an ethereal look that was belied only by her half smile.

Luke swallowed. *Dear God, it had been a long time since Peggy had looked at him and smiled.*

"I didn't think I'd find you out here," she said quietly, stepping along the path by the runner beans and looking at the plants rather than him.

Though he was tempted to reply immediately, Luke hesitated.

This was all very strange. Oh, not strange that he wanted her company. There wasn't a single situation in which he would not crave Peggy's company. The strange thing was that she appeared to desire his.

Perhaps desire was too strong a word. But surely she had seen him here in the kitchen gardens. That had been her chance to turn around and leave. He never would have noticed her.

And yet she hadn't. Instead of turning and exploring a different part of the garden, she had decided to enter. To speak, to gain his attention.

It was most unusual.

Stay calm, Luke tried to counsel himself. *Speak only words that you have carefully considered. Don't just blurt out the first thing you—*

"I love kitchen gardens," he said, words tumbling from his lips. "They're one of the few places I feel safe."

Luke's shoulders slumped. *You absolute fool, what did you have to go and say that for? Now she's going to think you an absolute cretin!*

Peggy had shot him a rather curious glance. Possibly. Perhaps that was wishful thinking. "Safe?"

Luke opened his mouth, considered how he could make a bombastic statement to impress, then looked back at Peggy.

It was Peggy. His Peggy. He didn't have to impress her. He wasn't standing in a Society soiree, trying to ensure the *ton* maintained its opinion of him.

That he was a rake. A rogue. A wit.

Those labels kept people away and that had been what he'd wanted, once. But not with Peggy.

"My father . . ." Luke began.

Then stopped. He had never mentioned this to anyone. No hint had ever slipped through his lips. He'd never promised himself, as such, but it had felt dishonorable to speak of while his father lived and disrespectful after his parents had died.

"Your father loved kitchen gardens?" Peggy prompted.

Luke swallowed. "Not exactly."

What was she doing here? Delightful as it was to be blessed with Peggy's presence, and with the total absence of a certain viscount, Luke could not understand it. Had she not made it perfectly clear she had absolutely no interest in him? That in fact, she was most interested in never having to suffer his company again?

Luke watched as Peggy reached the end of the row of runner beans and started meandering around the fruit trees.

"My father sneezed in gardens," Luke said. Well, that was true. "He spent little time outdoors."

"But you did," Peggy said softly, examining a growing apple.

"The kitchen gardens at Ashcott Hall were my favorite place as a boy. Peaceful, and yet full of life." Hardly aware where the words were coming from, Luke allowed them to pour from him.

"Whenever I needed to escape, I would come here. Well, there—to *my* kitchen gardens. No one would think to look for me there, a place for servants and hard work. Sometimes it would be hours before I was found and that was usually by a gardener."

Try as he might, Luke was unable to speak without bitterness, but far less than he'd expected. What was it about sharing truths near midnight? Was it the darkness, the coolness of the air, the moonlight, something else that made bearing his broken heart somehow easier?

"Escape?" Peggy repeated, glancing over.

Luke grimaced but managed to smile. "Not escape, exactly, I—"

"You said it and you meant it." Her voice was soft, not censuring, but chastising. "Don't retell the story to me, Luke, just because you don't like the truth it holds. I know you too well. I know when you're preparing to lie."

Luke breathed a laugh as he stepped along the border of cut flowers, in Peggy's general direction. "Well, I suppose that's true enough."

A flicker of a smile appeared on Peggy's face, then it was gone.

Or had he dreamt it? Was this what they called moon madness? The desire to see particular things, only to have them disappear as soon as you think you've caught sight of them?

Luke paused as he reached the end of the border. Peggy was no more twenty feet from him. He had reached the path that would take him to her, but he was not sure if she would welcome the closeness.

So he stopped and did something he almost never did. He revealed a little of himself.

"You never met my father," Luke said, swallowing as his throat grew dry. "He was a difficult man. A determined man, determined to have a son just like him. A son who cared little for the world, who spoke swiftly and with wit—"

"A son like you," Peggy said. She was leaning against the

trunk of the apple tree now.

Luke hesitated. "A son like what I was molded to become."

How was he saying this? Even when he and Peggy had been entirely in tune with each other, he had never considered revealing this to her. How strange that it was only now, when they were nothing to each other, that he could tell her.

Peggy's eyes widened. "You mean all this brashness, this coldness in company—"

"All learned, I'm afraid. And it turns out it's rather difficult to unlearn," said Luke with a wry laugh that sounded odd in the night. "It was considered uncouth by my father to show what he would call feminine emotions. To show weakness, as he called it."

He could still remember the lecture now, the same monologue he was treated to every time he showed partiality for one of the hunting dogs, or kindness to a servant, or sadness when struggling with something in the school room.

"You will be a duke someday, and I hope by God that by the time they put me in the ground, you've learned some control! To be a duke is one of the best things in the world and you, Luke Beauchamp, will not disgrace me!"

There appeared to be a rather inconvenient knot in Luke's throat that was preventing him from speaking.

"Luke?"

When had Peggy started calling him that again, Luke wondered. He had only just noticed that the formal title "Ashcott" had been dropped by her. Why?

"You don't want to hear all this—I am sorry. I-I should not have burdened you with . . . good evening, Lady Margaret," Luke said stiffly.

He turned to leave. *He should never have started talking about all this,* he thought. *It was all—*

"You don't have to go."

Luke froze, then turned slowly back to the grove of fruit trees.

Even in the silvery light of the moon, he could see Peggy flushing. Her cheeks were pink, her neck clearly warm, and her décolletage—but he shouldn't be looking there. Luke hastily dragged his gaze back to her face, which was still hot.

He could hardly believe it, but something had changed between them. Something he could not have planned or orchestrated. Was it the power of the kitchen garden? Or was Peggy finally accepting there was something between them, after all this time?

"Your father sounds like a hard man."

"He was. And yet it was the way he was raised, too," Luke admitted, brushing a hand along the foliage to steady himself, connect him to the ground. "I cannot blame him entirely."

"But he has made it impossible—well, near impossible, at any rate," Peggy said, her voice soft. "Impossible for you to speak of your heart."

The heart she spoke of skipped a beat. Luke unconsciously raised a hand to his chest.

It is yours, he wanted to say. *It's yours. It has been for—forever. Since I knew how to give it.*

But he couldn't say those words. He knew what response he would receive and he couldn't bear to suffer through it all over again. He had ached enough.

"I suppose nobles like myself aren't supposed to be able to speak of such things," Luke said, as nonchalantly as he could manage. "After all, no gentleman is encouraged to be open."

"It doesn't stop some."

Luke accidently broke the stem of a dahlia.

Of course it didn't stop some. Some like Lord Castor, he'd be bound. Now there was a man who had evidently been adored as a child, praised with no restrictions, no thrashings. Oh yes, Luke was certain it was very easy for men like that to spout their nonsense.

And had he? Though he desperately wanted to ask, he knew Peggy owed him nothing. She would not tell him whether Castor had already made his addresses to her.

But then—if he had, what was she doing entertaining a late-night conversation with him in the kitchen gardens?

Hope flickered in Luke. *She was not so far gone with Castor, then.*

"That's a dahlia."

Luke nodded. "Devotion."

"I-I beg your pardon?"

All too late, he realized his error. Luke turned and smiled, trying to show her it was not his own thought, but the flower's. *Well, that sounded ridiculous.*

"It's the language of flowers," he said quietly.

Peggy frowned. She was still standing by the apple tree, almost as though it were the safe place in a game of tag. "Language of flowers?"

"I discovered it in France—it's particularly popular there, all the gentlemen use it," said Luke, the knot in his throat starting to ease.

That was it—talk about something other than your terrible childhood, Ashcott.

Peggy was still frowning. "In France? What happened there?"

Luke drew himself up. Now wasn't the time to talk about the brutality he had seen, but flowers—there was a topic he could talk about. "It's as you say, some gentlemen are comfortable talking to the ladies, and some—"

"Are not," Peggy interrupted, looking pointedly at him.

Luke attempted to ignore that, though his stomach lurched. "They've created a system where different flowers have different meanings. A whole other language, if you will. So if you want to send a message to someone you admire, you merely create a bouquet with the right words. The right flowers."

The frown had disappeared from Peggy's face, the light of interest in her eyes. "Each flower with its own meaning. Yes, I believe I've heard of some in the *ton* who use flowers in such a way. But I suppose the French language of flowers is different?"

Though Luke had thought this neutral topic would be something to calm the conversation, his pulse was inexplicably racing.

"Each flower and each color has a meaning," he said, glancing at the bed of flowers. "For example, a red rose—"

"For love, surely."

Luke stared at Peggy. "Is it the same in England, then? You . . . well, I didn't expect you to have them all memorized."

That was one of the things he could not comprehend about this woman. Her intellect was as rapid and as voracious as any man's. She had only heard about the French language of flowers nigh on a minute ago, and it turned out she already knew the English equivalent off by heart?

Peggy's smile was shy. It caused a frisson up Luke's spine. "It just seemed obvious. And the aster?"

"Patience," said Luke with a rueful smile. "Not something I am known for."

Their mingled laughter did something strange to his fingers. They were tingling, as though at any moment he would be blessed enough to place them on Peggy's skin.

Oh God, this is what their life should have been, Luke could not help but think. A late-night walk in the kitchen gardens and laughter. He hadn't wanted much. Just her.

"Lily of the valley for sweetness, the chrysanthemum for innocence," Luke said, a smile slipping across his face. "The violet for wisdom."

"Not something I am known for," said Peggy quietly. "I think."

There was something so vulnerable in the way that she spoke, Luke hardly knew where to look.

Not known for wisdom? Peggy?

He would have said she was one of the wisest people he knew. It had been she, after all, who had known what the best course of action was for the two of them. Even if he had entirely mistaken the situation and regretted it ever since.

Perhaps it was that guilt which made him say what he said

next. "I never sent you flowers."

Luke thought his words would make Peggy bolt. She certainly straightened up for a moment as though to walk away, but then she leaned back once more against the apple tree.

"No," she said softly, her eyes meeting his. "No, you did not."

"I shall have to add that to my list of regrets," Luke said, once he was able to force words to emerge. "It's a long list, I'm afraid."

"And . . . and it's too late, of course," Peggy said, in a bracing manner. "You'll have no wish to do so now."

Luke stared.

He had expected anger, bitterness, a painful remark on how he had been a lax wooer at the best of times and now she was tired of his company. That was the Peggy he had known at the Sedleys' from the moment she had arrived. He had not expected this fragile creature. This vulnerable woman, standing there, talking about how he would not wish to send her flowers with such . . . such sadness.

Luke swallowed. Something had happened or was happening—he was not sure which. Something between them had altered. *Was it possible that she was tiring, finally, of Castor?*

"Well, if I were so fortunate as to send you a bouquet," Luke said with a dry laugh, "I know what I would include in it now."

"You do?"

Luke hesitated. Peggy's voice was eager, but he could not tell if this was the impulse of a moment or something truly deep within her. What if she regretted this tomorrow? What if this tolerance of his presence was due to tiredness—fading in the sun like the morning dew?

Still, he would never get a better chance. He had to take it.

"Carnations, of course," Luke said.

Peggy raised an eyebrow. "For . . .?"

"L-Love." *Damnit, why did his damned voice*—"Like roses, but more creative."

Her face was impassive. Oh, how he longed for her to smile, nod, say anything!

"Forget-me-nots," said Luke, hardly daring to breathe as he took a step to the fruit trees. "Because I would never want you to forget what we shared. If only . . . if only for a time."

Peggy said nothing, but she did not retreat as he advanced. Luke had to take that as encouragement, didn't he?

"Larkspur, for the bonds love brings," Luke said quietly, taking another step. "Because these bonds have never broken. Not for me, Peg."

She did not correct him and Luke's hopes soared as he took another step. *Oh, this was wonderful! This was everything he had hoped for!*

"Ivy for friendship. I'd want us—I want us to be friends, Peggy." Still she did not correct him, and Luke grew in boldness as he stepped closer. "Friendship with you would still be far more than I deserve, I know—"

"And what else?" Peggy asked quietly.

He was only a foot away. Luke could hardly tell how he had managed to get so close, but his attention had been entirely fixed on Peggy's eyes. Eyes which glittered in the moonlight.

With what? Unshed tears—of sorrow? Of joy?

"Tulips. For forgiveness. The forgiveness I hope, though don't expect, you'll give me." Luke tried to smile. "I-I am sorry, Peg."

She just looked at him—but she did not move away.

"And . . ." Luke swallowed. *There was no going back now.* "And myrtle."

"Myrtle?" Peggy repeated, gazing up.

She could have left. She could have walked away, flinched at his presence, but she hadn't. She wanted him, Luke knew with a spark of desire. And he would give her what she wanted.

"Myrtle," Luke said, lowering his voice and lips to hers. *Closer.* "For marriage."

"Marriage?"

Their lips were a mere inch apart, and Luke could have cried out as he moved—

"There you are! I thought I saw you sneak off into the gardens, and I thought—oh."

Luke rested his head for a moment, just a heartbeat, on Peggy's shoulder. Did she feel the same frustration he did? Was she similarly disappointed they had been disturbed?

And by that man, of all people!

But Luke ensured he was smiling as he plucked an apple from the tree and leaned back, offering it to Peggy. "There you go, Lady Margaret. The apple, as you requested."

Peggy's eyes were wide, though with fear they had been caught, frustration they had not been able to share a kiss, or relief they had not, Luke could not tell.

Castor beamed as he approached. "Ah, fruit picking in moonlight. How . . . interesting."

Luke gritted his teeth and managed not to say anything. *Of all the ill-timed, ill-mannered—could the man not see they had been busy?*

"But it is getting chilly, Lady Margaret, and we would not wish for you to catch a summer cold," the idiot was saying.

"You're quite right, of course," said Luke formally. "Here."

His last word was spoken in harmony with Castor as they both offered an arm.

Luke watched Peggy look between them. Well, he had offered her as much of an apology as he could make. It had cost him. Baring his soul like that, it was difficult. But he had done it. Now all he could do was hope she would choose—

"Th-Thank you, Lord Castor," Peggy said quietly as she took the viscount's arm. "It is a little cold. Perhaps . . . perhaps going inside would be best."

Luke tried not to look at Castor's wide smile.

"Come on then, my dear," the viscount said smoothly.

Luke expected—well, hoped—Peggy would chastise the endearment. It was astonishingly intimate, particularly for a man who had only met her a few days ago.

But she said nothing. And so Luke was forced to walk, silently, behind the pair who strode forward arm-in-arm, all the way back to the house.

CHAPTER TWELVE

26 August, 1811

P EGGY KNEW WHAT she should do. She knew the minute the
door opened.

She should leave.

You are not to be trusted, she thought as she watched the tall
figure of Luke Beauchamp, Duke of Ashcott step—again—into
the library. *That is a man around whom you have no control!*

Last night was a perfect example. She should have left the
kitchen gardens the moment she'd seen it was Luke, Peggy knew.
But she hadn't. And the worst of it all was . . . she couldn't find
any regret within her.

Even when he had spoken so painfully about his father.

Even when he had spoken so powerfully about the language
of flowers.

Even when he had come so passionately close to—

She'd never know. Lord Castor had interrupted them.

And a good thing too, Peggy tried to tell herself as she dragged
her gaze away from the handsome—from the *intruding* man
before her, and back to her book. Why, if Lord Castor had
stumbled across them but a minute later, her reputation would be
ruined, and Luke would be forced by the rules of propriety to

marry her.

A shiver rushed up her spine. *And would that be such a bad thing?*

Peggy pushed the thought away as resolutely as she could. *Yes. Yes, it would.* Because when Luke had proposed last year, it had been from a place of love and devotion. Did she really wish to—to entrap him now into a marriage without any of those things?

"Larkspur, for the bonds love bring. Because these bonds have never broken. Not for me, Peg."

"Ah," said Luke, suddenly spotting her in the large armchair by the window. "Ah."

"Ah," said Peggy helplessly, her tongue utterly useless.

It had become increasingly difficult to act rational around Luke since overhearing his conversation with the Duke of Sedley. Words and phrases kept echoing in her mind, making it challenging to pay attention to what the Luke before her was saying.

"My biggest regret. A regret I'll never escape. I'll spend the rest of my life, Sedley, knowing that I should be by that woman's side. And I'm forever barred from it. And blast it all, for good reason."

Discomfort prickled her lungs. How was she supposed to sit when she was around a man she had once loved and for whom she now felt . . . felt something. Something strange. How was one supposed to—to breathe?

When had breathing become so difficult, anyway?

Peggy tried to smile. *This was ridiculous.* She was in the library reading, and he had entered the library in search, no doubt, of a book. There was nothing untoward here. Nothing conniving. She certainly wasn't imagining him pulling her to her feet, pushing her against a bookcase, and—

"I am reading a book," Peggy announced, mostly to disrupt the scandalous images in her mind.

Luke blinked. "Yes. Good."

Only too late did Peggy realize just how idiotic her words were.

Honestly. She was reading a book? Why not point out that the sky was blue, or that books were made of paper, or that she . . . she felt peculiar whenever she was around him. Almost like when he had first spoken to her at Almack's, and she hadn't known what to do with her hands, and—

And she had not known then, Peggy realized with a sinking feeling, *what she knew now. That she was falling in love with him.*

Then. Not now. Obviously.

"I thought I would read a book," said Luke, gesturing aimlessly around at the bookshelves, absolutely jammed with books. "If I can find one."

Peggy stared. Was it possible—surely it was impossible—that Luke could sense her discomfort? Was that why he was speaking in such a stilted voice? Or perhaps, even worse, did he regret what he'd said last night? It had been late and the moonlight played funny tricks on the eyes sometimes. Was it possible it had played funny tricks with his heart?

Peggy swallowed. *This was madness.* She was no young chit just entering Society. She had full control over her faculties. She was not in love. She was a little in lust, but that was a natural reaction to being around Luke Beauchamp, more's the pity.

But she was not in love. Most definitely not. She'd stopped all that nonsense last year.

"What . . . what sort of book are you looking for?" Peggy asked aloud.

Yes, that was it. Keep to neutral, calm—

"Not a romance, I think," Luke said with an awkward smile. "More than enough of that around here."

Heat scalded Peggy's cheeks. And this was why she could never seriously consider Luke as a suitor again: his inability to be serious for two days together. Why, yesterday he was spouting nonsense about forgiveness, and love, and—

"Myrtle. For marriage."

"Marriage?"

Try as she might, Peggy's cheeks simply would not calm

down. Ignoring them completely and hoping Luke would do her the courtesy of doing the same, she said, "Well, there are plenty of other books in here. I'm reading about France."

She held up the book, as though he would be able to see the title from the other side of the room and instantly realized her mistake. As though the gesture had been an invitation, Luke stepped across the library and settled on the sofa opposite her armchair.

"So I see," he said softly.

Peggy swallowed. She had not actually intended him to come closer. For some reason, every foot Luke advanced nearer to her increased her temperature by about five degrees.

And most irritating it was, too.

But it had given her the opportunity to ask a question that had been lingering in her mind for some time, ever since she had literally walked into him on the streets of Bath. The moment she realized he was back in England.

"What was it like?" Peggy said quietly. "France, I mean."

It was not a question she would ask just anyone. There was little Peggy had personally experienced about war, but she had seen some of the men who had returned without limbs, eyes bandaged, their spirits broken on the battlefields against Napoleon.

Luke may look whole, but she was no fool. That did not necessarily mean—

"Why?" asked Luke roughly.

Peggy bit her lip and opened up her book. "It doesn't—never mind."

She tried to concentrate on the words on the page but she could not take them in. Just when she thought they might be able to return to some sort of cordiality, she was able to destroy it.

"I . . . I'm sorry."

Peggy was astonished. Luke looked genuinely regretful. "I beg your pardon?"

"Don't make me say it again, Peg," Luke said softly.

Peggy swallowed. She had been vehement about being addressed in the proper way by this man, but now, in this conversation . . . it did not seem right, somehow, to correct him.

She let it pass. This once.

"I am the one who should apologize," she said awkwardly. "I should not have asked—"

"You can ask me anything you want," Luke said, interrupting her with a shrug. "I cannot promise to answer, of course."

Peggy opened her mouth, hesitated, then closed it again.

It was all too easy to see meaning in Luke's words where there was none. He did not mean—he could not mean he was happy for her to ask him *anything*. He meant about France.

Still. It was a tempting thought.

"I . . . I don't really know what to ask," Peggy admitted with a dry laugh.

There was another laugh, but it wasn't from Luke. She could see through the window behind him that Lord Castor and Miss Yates were taking a walk along the gravel path. Well, hopefully that would resolve that problem. If the two of them could form an attachment, she would be free to—

To do nothing, Peggy cut off that thought. It was not as though she had any alternatives. She was not going to allow Luke to— she couldn't . . .

Luke glanced over his shoulder. When he turned back, his expression was wooden. "Castor distracting you?"

"No!" Peggy said automatically, then breathed an awkward laugh. "Well, yes. I do apologize. I—I want to hear about France. Anything you want to tell me."

He looked to be in two minds as to whether or not to even stay in the library, but then Luke took a deep breath and leaned back on the sofa.

"I hadn't ever thought I would go there during the war," he said softly, a wry smile creeping over his face. "Until I was given marching orders by your brother, of course."

Peggy nodded, but said nothing. The less said about that, the better.

"It was astonishing. In some ways, France was precisely the same as it was when I went on my Grand Tour," said Luke quietly, his smile fading. "And in some ways entirely different. There is great distrust there. Great fear. Nobles like ourselves are in danger at every turn, yet there is still some sort of strange respect for us. One has to be careful."

Peggy stared, transfixed. She had never heard anyone talk about France, not like this. "I didn't manage to spot which regiment you'd joined."

Was it her imagination, or did Luke look amused? She had not intended it as a jest.

"That would be because I . . . well, I didn't join a regiment."

Peggy frowned. "Then . . ."

Her voice trailed away as she looked into the dark eyes and perceptive smile of the man she had once known better than any other. In a way, perhaps she still did.

It was only then, seated opposite him in the library of a beautiful English manor, hundreds of miles from France, that Peggy realized what function Luke had performed there.

"You . . ." Peggy licked her lips, trying not to notice Luke's focus. "You were a spy?"

The very idea seemed absurd. Luke Beauchamp, Duke of Ashcott, was a rake! A scoundrel, a philanderer. He had been well known as a seducer of young ladies when she had met him, and though she had never given him all of her, Peggy knew quite well that he was a man well skilled in those particular arts. And that was all Society thought of him. Now she knew it was a cover he had invented as a boy to satisfy his father: a manly man, one who did not give consideration to his conquests. No weakness, no feminine emotions, was that not what he had said?

But the idea that Luke could be a spy . . .

"Your words," Luke said gently. "Not mine."

Peggy found herself leaning forward. "But I am right, aren't I?"

"Let's just say I performed some services to the Crown while I was in France that were not noted down on any dispatches," said Luke delicately. "Nor will you find them written in any formal reports. As far as I know, there never was any paperwork."

Peggy stared. The knowledge Luke had taken his very life into his hands in France to serve his country had always impressed her. She would challenge anyone not to be impressed!

But to do so under the pretense of just being in France for the sake of it—no uniform, nor presumably any weapons to protect him? No one by his side, no brother officers or regiment to stand alongside him?

Admiration for him rose unbidden, along with something Peggy had not expected.

Pride.

But that was ridiculous. He was hardly hers to be proud of!

"You must have seen real danger," Peggy said softly.

Luke shrugged.

"I know that look," she said with a giggle. "That means you did—don't try to lie to me, Luke. I told you last . . . last night. I know when you're lying."

Their gazes met and Peggy gasped at the intensity in Luke's eyes. If she did not know any better, she'd think he wished to say something. Something most disgraceful. Something he should not say.

She watched him swallow, watched the tension tauten across his jaw as Luke considered her.

"I saw danger," Luke said eventually, his voice low. "But it was nothing to the danger I would have been in had I stayed here."

I want you gone—from London, from England.

Her brother's words flashed across Peggy's memory, making every breath difficult.

She knew Henry well. As far as she knew, the man had never lifted a hand to anyone, not even a fly. He would never have actually hurt Luke.

"My brother's threats should never be taken seriously," Peggy began.

"It wasn't your brother I was worried about," said Luke. "No offense, of course."

She frowned, fingers tightening around the book still in her lap. "Then . . . then what were you afraid of?"

"You," Luke said simply.

Peggy's mouth fell open. "What? You cannot be—me?"

What on earth was the man talking about? She was hardly like—like Lady Romeril, who was feared throughout Society as a doyenne who could make or break a reputation. She wasn't even someone like Minny. Her sister-in-law had the physical strength so many men didn't—she'd seen the woman lift a barrel!

So why had Luke been afraid of her?

Her confusion was clearly still evident on her face, for Luke chuckled. "Well, not you precisely. More . . . more of what I would do around you. Of the power you had over me. Of the pain I knew I would feel if you were to listen to your brother and break off our engagement."

"You broke it," Peggy pointed out, chest tight.

"Only because I knew I couldn't bear it if you did so," Luke said quietly. "It was pathetic. Foolish. But I did it, all the same."

It was impossible not to stare.

Was that the truth? Peggy had considered the matter over and over in her mind for so long, it was sometimes difficult to recall what had actually happened and what were the twisted, pained images she had concocted.

Was it true Luke had only stormed out, only ended an engagement which had only existed for mere minutes, because he believed *she* would do so?

Try as she might, Peggy could not see a hint of falsehood in Luke's face. He had always been such an open book to her, but now she could not tell. Was it only wishful thinking on her part, or was there real veracity in his words?

"Well," said Peggy, deciding she would attempt to discern it later, when not faced with the intoxicating presence of Luke himself. "France is a long way to go to forget me!"

She had intended the words as a joke as she settled back in her armchair, yet Luke looked serious.

"A very long way. And it didn't even work."

An odd feeling was filling the library. A delicate calm Peggy had never felt before. An awkward happiness, a resolute relief that was unfamiliar. A sort of . . . truce?

Peggy could not understand it, but she also could not look away. Luke had some hold over her, she could no longer deny it. No matter how much she tried to convince herself she had no feelings for him, there was something inside her that simply would not let him go.

And that was why, Peggy thought sternly, *she had to say something. She had to put an end to this, once and for all.* She couldn't spend the rest of her life wondering.

"You . . . you know it would never have worked between us, Luke," Peggy whispered.

She had intended to speak more boldly, but somehow the words had emerged from her lips almost as a plaintive cry.

Luke did not look away, nor did he look angry. He merely murmured, "Why not?"

"Why not?" Peggy repeated.

There was a tingling in her shoulder blades she could not explain.

Why? Why?

"Because—well, because it didn't," said Peggy, attempting to be rational. "We clearly can't resolve arguments together without one of us storming off—"

"I agree, we'd have to work on that," said Luke calmly.

Peggy's eyes widened. *Was he truly—was he really trying to convince her?*

Why was she letting him? How could she allow herself to be captivated by him again, just when she had been so certain she had finally rid her mind of Luke Beauchamp?

Another laugh through the window. *It appeared Miss Yates and Lord Castor were getting on well, Peggy* thought. Far better than she and Luke were managing, at any rate.

"You—you would have tired of me eventually," Peggy said, a bit more firmly this time. "And—"

"I don't think that's possible," Luke said seriously. "I think you would be more likely to grow tired of my coldness. My inability to express my weakness. My weakness for you."

"You would have learned, over time, I would have helped— that's not the point!" Peggy blustered.

Goodness, was she starting to try to convince him now? What was going on?

"I think our faults could have been overcome with love and affection," Luke was saying with a shrug. "Can you think of a single thing that might have come between us which could not?"

Peggy's mind was whirling so fast, it was impossible to think of a single word.

Why was he pushing this? Did he truly think she was going to change her mind? That the last year or so could be wiped from her mind, forgotten and never considered again?

It was foolish to stay here. The moment Luke had entered the library, she should have departed. But Peggy had not, and now she was pinned to this armchair by the sheer force of his determination that they would have been happy.

Happy. Together.

"It wouldn't have worked," Peggy said softly, unable to look at him any longer. She looked at the book she was clasping. "It just . . . you know it wouldn't, Luke. Maybe . . . perhaps it's best this way."

He did not reply yet she could not bring herself to look at him. This was it, then. This was the end. She had never thought they would ever be able to have a rational conversation about it, but apparently they could.

And all it took was a passionate kiss, some extremely sensual conversation, and a moonlight walk through a kitchen garden.

"Well," said Luke's bracing voice. "If I can't have you for a wife—"

His wife. She could have been his wife.

"—then can we at least be friends?"

Tears threatened the corners of her eyes. *Friends?* After everything they had shared, after what he had been to her, the dreams she had built around him, dreams that would never see the light of day, he wanted to be friends?

"Ivy for friendship. I'd want us—I want us to be friends, Peggy. Friendship with you would still be far more than I deserve, I know—"

Peggy forced the tears back. *This was what you wanted,* she reminded herself. *You are not in love with Luke Beauchamp, Duke of Ashcott—and now it appears he is willing to stop loving you! This is perfect!*

So why did it feel as though the world was ending?

"Of—of course," Peggy said, making herself look up. There was an odd look in Luke's face, but it disappeared as their eyes met. "Friends. Yes."

Luke nodded briskly. "Well, friend, I think it's high time I did what I came in here to do."

Peggy's breath caught in her throat. *Was he about to kiss her?*

"Which book on France would you recommend?"

All the tension that had built up in her chest suddenly melted away. "B-Book?"

That was why he came to the library in the first place, you dolt.

"I think I'll start with this one," Luke said, easily leaning across from the sofa and plucking a very dull looking book from a shelf. "Enjoy your book."

Peggy blinked. "En—Enjoy my—oh, yes. Enjoy yours."

But Luke did not reply. He had already opened up to the first page and begun perusing its contents.

She had to say something. Surely they could not just remain like this, doing nothing, saying nothing of meaning? But what to say, which had not already been said? Except . . .

Peggy swallowed. Except how she actually felt about him.

Those were words she had promised herself would never slip through her lips. But she couldn't lie to herself any longer. She cared for Luke, cared for him beyond what was reasonable.

And they were alone.

Peggy cleared her throat. She jolted as Luke immediately looked up. "Luke . . . Luke, I—"

"There you two are! Found them!" cried Mrs. Marnion cheerfully, careering into the library with a wide grin. "We need another two for whist, and I knew you'd be—but you're reading."

Peggy simply stared at the woman. *Of all the ill-timed—*

"It is a library," pointed out Luke calmly.

"Reading? At a house party, when there is so much festivity to be had?" Mrs. Marnion looked absolutely astonished. "I've never heard of such a thing!"

Just for a moment, Peggy caught Luke's eye and they shared a smile. It shot through her like an arrow then it was gone. As though she had dreamed it. As though it had never been.

"Whist," Mrs. Marnion said with great authority, "is a most sociable and acceptable game. We've got a table set up in the Orangery."

Peggy could see by the expression on the woman's face that she would brook no argument. And that could only mean . . .

"Yes, Lord Braedon and I have set up a table," said Mrs. Marnion, confirming all of Peggy's suspicions. "And that Miss Yates and Lord Castor were supposed to be joining us, but they've disappeared off somewhere. And I don't want to be left alone with Lord Brae—I mean, whist really needs four players. But now you're here. Come along!" she commanded.

"Isn't the Orangery absolutely boiling?" asked Luke mildly, putting down his book and rising.

Peggy watched him with astonishment. He wasn't going to actually permit this to occur, was he? The Orangery would indeed be baking in this weather. It would be like stepping onto the sun!

"You don't mind the heat, do you?" he asked, turning to her

and offering his arm.

It did not appear to matter whether she was in the Orangery or not—Peggy was being slowly dipped into a boiling heat, regardless. The fervor was rising up her legs, past her waist, and would surely be boiling her face in a minute if she were not careful. If she did not look away from that quizzical brow, those laughing eyes.

Mrs. Marnion still stood in the library doorway, but somehow, Peggy felt emboldened. Why shouldn't she speak as boldly to Luke as he did to her?

They were friends now, after all.

"Oh, I can stand a little heat, if you are competent enough to challenge me," Peggy said, lifting her chin courageously. "The question is, can you?"

"I think I know how to warm you," said Luke quietly.

And that did it. Peggy had hoped her cheeks would not pink, that the color rising through her chest would stop at her neck, but she was much disappointed.

Or not disappointed. She could hardly tell. The walls of the library seemed to be closing in, blocking out all life beyond their walls, even Mrs. Marnion, until only they were left.

Was this . . . was he flirting with her?

Dear God, was she flirting back?

"I . . . I think you do," stammered Peggy, taking a step forward with no idea why she was doing so. "The question is, will you?"

Will you?

It was an innocent question. *Fine,* Peggy thought furiously, *not quite innocent.*

But it was one she would dearly love answered. He did not look away. It was as though Mrs. Marnion had ceased to exist.

Almost.

"I am confused—are we playing whist, or not?"

Luke chuckled at Mrs. Marnion's plaintive question. "We're certainly playing something, aren't we, Peggy?"

Peggy hesitated.

"If I can't have you for a wife, then can we at least be friends?"

Just minutes ago, Luke had wished to be her friend. If he'd wanted to be more, he would have said, would he not? After that passionate kiss, after all he had said in the kitchen garden, he had evidently resigned himself to nothing more than good terms with her.

Good terms? With the man she—

She wasn't even going to think it.

The point was that Luke merely wished to be friends. And all this flirtatious talk would simply end in tears. Hers, probably.

"We are playing whist—a short game, Mrs. Marnion," Peggy said aloud, finally breaking the connection with Luke. "And—"

"Oh, don't bother, I'm sure," said Mrs. Marnion with a snip in her voice. "I didn't come here to beg for players. I will find my Mr. Marnions, they will rescue me from Lord Brae—I mean, accompany me. Good afternoon."

And she was gone.

Luke turned to Peggy. For a moment, she was convinced he was going to say something... something wonderful. An admission of affection, a joke at Mrs. Marnion's expense they could both laugh at. Perhaps he would even—

But he merely raised an eyebrow, dropped her arm, and returned to his seat and book. "What a most interesting interlude."

"Yes," Peggy said hoarsely. She swallowed. "Most interesting."

Silence fell in the library and Peggy knew, from that moment, that she had lost her one chance at being honest with Luke. She had lost him.

CHAPTER THIRTEEN

27 August, 1811

"—REALLY MUST RETIRE to bed," the Duchess of Sedley was saying with a wide yawn. "Goodness, I just can't seem to keep my eyes open at the moment!"

"Well, there's no reason for that, is there?" said her husband with a wide smile.

Luke glanced between them. Really, if they were hoping to make a big announcement in the autumn, that opportunity was gone. It could not be more obvious the duchess was expecting.

Still. It wasn't so bad, seeing the connection they shared.

A twinge made him struggle for breath, just for a moment.

Envy was not an emotion he regularly suffered. It was difficult to feel envy when one was a duke. The Dukedom of Ashcott, in particular, was known for its wealth, extensive lands, and an art collection even Luke had to admit was rather fine. Even if he couldn't tell the difference between a Gainsborough and a Turner.

So it was not often that Luke saw someone and knew, right in the pit of his stomach, that he wanted what they had.

He watched as Sedley touched his wife's arm. Just gently. Only a few inches of skin were actually connected, and only for a moment. But he could almost hear the rustle of affection between them. Luke shifted uncomfortably in his armchair and glanced about to see if anyone else had noticed. One person had. And of course, it was the one person whose arm he wanted to touch.

Everything had become so complicated since he had spoken those idiotic words.

"If I can't have you for a wife, then can we at least be friends?"

Peggy flushed as their eyes met and she immediately looked at the book in her hands. The same book she had been attempting to read yesterday when they had spoken in the library. When he had branded himself, perhaps forever, with the title he had never wanted from her in the first place.

Friend.

Luke would have groaned if it would not have attracted so much attention. The two Mr. Marnions were playing a game of chess to one side, and Miss Yates was working on some embroidery as she chatted blithely to Mrs. Marnion—or at least, she permitted Mrs. Marnion to chatter away to her. The two viscounts, Luke was delighted to see, were nowhere to be found. Playing billiards, most likely.

And good riddance, he couldn't help but think. The further away that Castor fellow stayed from him, the better.

But it appeared the Duchess of Sedley's imminent departure had caused something of a stir within the party.

"Oh, well if you think this is the appropriate time to retire, Your Grace, I will follow you," said Mrs. Marnion hurriedly, rising to her feet.

Luke watched the duchess smile. "My word, Mrs. Marnion. All the way to my bedchamber?"

Her gentle teasing caused a ripple of laughter across the room. Luke used it as an excuse to look at Peggy. She had not laughed. Why? Was her book so fascinating that she was, finally, lost in its pages? Or was she rather more distracted by something else? Him, perhaps?

You're a fool, Ashcott, Luke thought, determined to bring his errant thoughts under control. *After all this time, Peggy knows her own mind. She gratefully accepted your offer of friendship, did she not?*

You idiot. You should never have offered it.

"I think I will retire also," said Mrs. Marnion's husband.

Their son was outraged. "Only because I am about to win, Father!"

"Nonsense," was the confident reply. "Checkmate in four moves."

Luke smiled to watch the younger man fume. "But—but—"

"I believe I will to bed as well," said Miss Yates, carefully placing her embroidery on the console table to the right of the drawing room's fireplace. "My eyes grow weary, and I would prefer to continue with this later. Besides, I have a letter to read. Apparently there is growing gossip in London about the disappearance of Lady Genevieve Cotton-Powell, and I simply cannot miss it."

The vast majority of the company was drifting out. All of them, save—

"Lady Margaret," said Miss Yates lightly. "Will you accompany me to our corridor?"

Luke's gaze flickered over Peggy's face. He could read her far better than a book.

She wished to stay. And she did not wish to make a fuss about it.

Why? His body craved to know, really know, what was in that mind of hers. Oh, he could see clearly what she wanted, but not why. He was the only one here, but she had avoided at every opportunity the chance to be alone with him.

Peggy looked up.

Luke gasped, his breath caught in his lungs. *She wanted to speak to him.*

But it couldn't be—he had to be mistaken. It was wishful thinking again, a longing deep within his bones, which had never truly been satisfied the instant he'd walked away.

"I-I think I will stay a while longer," Peggy was saying to Miss

Yates in a quiet voice. "The light is perfectly sufficient for reading, and I want to know what happens next."

Luke swallowed.

He should not be seeing hints where there were none. He was only going to lead himself down a trail of nonsense, he knew, and when Peggy undoubtedly reminded him of his own words—that they should be friends—friends would have to be enough, Luke thought with a heavy sigh. Being friends with Peggy would still be an honor. And if what she needed was a friend, who was he to deny her?

By God, he loved her too much to deny her anything. Her happiness, wrought perhaps from a different source than he had wished, was still the most important thing in the world.

"—if you are sure," Miss Yates was saying.

She cast a look at Luke which was most uncomfortably keen, then curtseyed. The door closed quietly behind her . . . and they were alone.

Luke fought the instinct to immediately rise from his chair and move closer to Peggy.

They were already alone. How much more intimate could it be?

"You have had a good evening?" came Peggy's clear but soft voice.

Luke tried to smile, he really did. This was what being friends was, remember? But try as he might, he had never been able to picture a friendship between himself and Peggy until now. It was far too tame, too restrained for anything he wished to share with her.

"Good enough," he said gruffly.

"I thought you would wish to play billiards with the other gentlemen," said Peggy, closing her book and setting it aside. "With . . . with Lord Braedon. And Lord Castor."

Luke's fingers gripped the arms of his chair tightly.

Well, friends should be able to converse about one's future intended, should they not? Even if it made his head ring and lights pop in front of his eyes.

Lord Castor, indeed. The day he had to sit and watch that blackguard take Peggy's hand in marriage in a church was the day he would leave England for good.

But that, Luke thought, *was hardly the thought of a friend, was it?*

"Braedon is all very well," Luke said as easily as he could manage. "Though I suspect he'll get himself into a mischief one of these days. He's far too easily won and far too easily influenced."

Her smile was wry. "He'll fall in love with someone entirely unsuitable, I suppose."

His breath hitched in his chest. "Probably."

Like I fell in love with you, Luke wanted to say. *And I'm a damned duke. I'm not supposed to be utterly devoted to anyone. Or make myself vulnerable. Or make it so easy for someone—for you to hurt me.*

But he couldn't think like that. That was the past, wasn't it? A past he could never return to.

"Lord Castor, on the other hand," Luke began, hardly knowing where he was going. He paused, just for a moment. Being the bigger man was far more of a challenge than he had anticipated. Drawing on reserves of good manners Luke had not known he had, and pulling in as much of his genteel breeding as he could manage, he smiled. "Lord Castor is not a man I like."

Well, it was not the most auspicious start, but it was something.

Luke tried not to look at the way Peggy's cheeks were growing pinker. Blast, she was far more in love with that brute than she'd ever been with him. Look at the way her coloring changed so rapidly!

"But not liking a man does not make him a bad one," Luke continued, every word spoken as lightly as possible. "If . . . if you and he . . ."

The words died in his throat. Luke fell into silence, cursing his inability to speak plainly. Things had never been this difficult in France, and that had been in a war!

The fire in the grate was fading away. A log crackled, splitting and throwing up sparks. The light flickered across Peggy's face, accentuating her beauty.

Luke's stomach curdled. Was he the sort of man to wish misery on the person he loved, just because he could not make her happy? Was he truly that cruel?

He took a deep breath and met Peggy's curious expression. "If Lord Castor makes you happy, then I am content."

The words echoed in the following silence. Luke forced himself to let out the breath he had taken.

There. It was said.

And now Peggy knew he wished only the best for her—had, in fact, gone far beyond the expected duty of a friend to wish her well, even with a below average partner like Castor.

At least he would be able to hold his head up high, Luke thought bitterly. Though whether he could bring himself to attend their wedding was another matter.

Peggy rose. Her skirts, a soft green silk that seemed to shimmer blue with every movement, rustled as she stepped toward him at such a pace, Luke was astonished. She halted just before him, only a foot away.

There was a curious expression on her face. If Luke did not know any better, he would have said it was . . . anger?

"How dare you say that!" Peggy said in a low, furious voice. "How dare you!"

Luke stared.

She was magnificent. Her dark hair was haloed by the glowing fire behind her and there was true passion in her eyes which illuminated her face far greater than any blaze could. The silhouette of her form was doing something most uncomfortable to his nether regions, and the power in her voice—that was the sort of power that launched the attack on Troy.

But her words were most confusing. *How dare he?* How dare he praise the man she had evidently chosen to be her spouse? *What on earth was going on?*

"How dare you!" Peggy repeated, eyes narrowed.

"I-I—how dare I?" repeated Luke, utterly bewildered.

He rose in turn, as though by standing he could somehow explain himself. But why was he the one having to explain himself, when all he had done was attempt a politeness he had not truly felt?

"You!" Peggy said, reaching out a finger and poking him in the chest.

Luke's hand instinctively moved to the place she had touched—a place that burnt after the momentary contact.

"Me?" he repeated, completely lost. "All I said was—"

"You said that Lord Castor making me happy would make you content. How can you say that?" Peggy said, her voice cracking with emotion.

Luke had absolutely no idea how he'd managed to stumble into an argument, but he had obviously mortally offended. Perhaps she had misheard him. It was certainly a great distance, at least ten feet, between where they had been sitting.

"All I said was that if Castor made you happy, then that's a good thing," Luke said. "What's wrong with that—if his proposal has delighted you—"

"How can you speak of Lord Castor's proposal with such equanimity?" Peggy said, her dark eyes searching his.

Luke swallowed. He did not feel any equanimity now. "Because if it makes you happy—"

"It's you I'm in love with!"

And that was when the world halted.

Oh, it probably continued spinning on its axis. It probably kept making its way through the solar system around the sun, following the path set out for it by mathematics he had never truly understood and had quickly ceased to worry about.

But right here, in this drawing room, in this corner of England, Luke was certain everything had stopped. There was a strange ringing in his ears. Something had changed, irrevocably, and nothing he did or said would ever change it back. Not now.

Luke stared at Peggy. Her face was flushed, not from embarrassment but from passion. Or was he just seeing things he wished to see?

"You . . . you are in love with me?" Luke managed to repeat.

Peggy poked him, hard, once again. "I always have been, you absolute dolt!"

None of this made sense—Luke could not understand what was happening.

She loved him? Yes, once, a long time ago. What felt like a lifetime ago. But those feelings had naturally disappeared, had they not, after he had been such a fool as to walk away?

"But . . . but . . ." Luke swallowed and tried to get a hold of himself. *He was a gentleman. He was an Ashcott—a duke! He didn't stand before women who declared their affections for him and stammer!* "But you and Lord Castor—the way he spoke to you, the way you've been speaking to him—"

"Oh, it was just something to distract at first," said Peggy, waving a hand.

Luke's heart was thundering so heavily in his chest, it was a wonder she could not hear it. Perhaps she could. "Distract? From what?"

Another poke. "From you, you complete imbecile!"

But this time Peggy was not quick enough. Luke's hand reached forward and he captured hers, holding it tight.

And heat, passionate heat, flowed through them. Luke's breath quickened at the very physical reaction he had to such contact and he could see, almost hear, the similar change in Peggy.

They were standing but inches apart. How that had happened, Luke wasn't sure. They were alone in the drawing room, everyone else had retired to bed, and they—

They were arguing about how Peggy was in love with him.

Luke blinked. *No, that couldn't be right.*

"A distraction from me?" He had to get to the bottom of this. "I don't understand."

"Don't you?" Peggy asked. Her fingers had entwined themselves in his, unresisting, as though craving his touch. "Every moment I've been here I've been trying not to look at you, not to notice you. I needed a distraction. Something to stop me making a fool of myself!"

Her words were ringing in Luke's ears but they did not make sense. How could they? If Peggy needed to be distracted, that could only mean—

"You wanted to make me jealous?" Luke said, with dawning comprehension.

The guilt in Peggy's eyes told him the truth before her lips did. "Only at first, and then—oh, Luke. If only he hadn't interrupted us in the kitchen gardens."

Luke's manhood twitched.

"Forget-me-nots. Because I would never want you to forget what we shared. If only . . . if only for a time."

"I didn't think you wanted me to kiss you against that apple tree," he breathed, unable to look away from those dazzling eyes.

Peggy smiled. "Was it an apple tree? I didn't notice."

Luke groaned, lowering his head only briefly so his forehead touched hers, before straightening up. He couldn't lose control, not now. Not when, finally, it appeared he and Peggy were about to understand each other.

"Just to be absolutely clear," he said hastily. "You're in love with me. Not with the Viscount Castor."

"Do you think I'd be standing here like this, waiting for you to kiss me," asked Peggy quietly, "if I were in love with another man?"

Dimly, he knew he should probably feel a little angry, a little piqued. It was not pleasant to think Peggy had only entertained the attentions of that rogue because she'd been so concerned she would fall into his arms. But Castor was a part of the past now. Their shared past, in a way. Evidence, as though they had needed more, that they were not very good at staying away from each other. Besides, Luke's relief that Peggy had absolutely no affections for the viscount delighted him more than he could say.

So he didn't say. He moved.

As it turned out, he barely needed to. Peggy stepped into his arms, lifting up her lips for his kiss, and Luke moaned as he captured her mouth with his.

It was like . . . not quite like coming home, because she had already been his home—his only home—for a great deal of time. It was more like the world was being put to rights. Or as though he had been starved for months and was finally being offered the most splendid spread. And nothing could tear him away from the quivering anticipation that rushed through him as she parted her lips and welcomed him in.

And by God, Luke took what he had craved for so long. His fingers swiftly moved not to her waist—no, they moved far past her waist to her buttocks, cupping the heavy warmth of her behind and trying not to moan as he did so.

As his tongue explored her delicious mouth, Luke was vaguely aware of Peggy's hands scrabbling at his cravat, one of her legs lifted slightly so that she brought his hips, his manhood, closer to her core.

As their kisses became more frantic, fervor increasing with each one, Luke knew he could never be parted from her now. Not now he knew she loved him. Not now she had been vulnerable, and open, and revealed just how desperately she had attempted to forget him.

An unsuccessful task, in the end. *Thank God.*

Luke fairly whimpered as his cravat was removed and his fingers started scrabbling at Peggy's skirts. All he wanted to do was feel her skin—

"Oh, Christ."

He should have known or, at the very last, guessed. It had been so humid of late, it was no wonder that she wasn't wearing any stockings. And Peggy's stockingless legs were so soft, her thigh shivering as Luke's finger trailed along it, glorying in the intimacy.

And then she broke their kiss.

"I-I think," Peggy breathed, her nose stroking his own, her lips tantalizingly out of reach. "I think we should go up now."

Luke moaned, disappointment pooling in his stomach. *Go up?* The last thing he wanted to do now was bid Peggy goodnight and go upstairs to his cold, empty, and Peggy-less bedchamber. How could she suggest such a thing?

"God, do we have to?" he asked miserably.

CHAPTER FOURTEEN

"I-I THINK," PEGGY said, every part of her desperate to continue what they had started. How was it possible that she was still able to speak? "I think we should go up now."

Excitement welled in her chest. After such confusion, misunderstanding, arguments, after thinking they would never find common ground again—finally, they could be together.

Luke groaned, and his head dropped. "God, do we have to?"

Peggy's excitement immediately dissipated as his words echoed in her mind.

What had she done? Embarrassed herself utterly. Shamed her name, her family, and herself. Given in to all the desires she had attempted to keep to herself for so long. Revealed herself to be nothing but a desperate woman, not even desired enough by this man—a man she was throwing herself at.

Did they have to? Was that really what Luke thought about the prospect of them making love?

Peggy released herself from his disappointed grip and tried not to think of what she had already shared with the man who was now, it appeared, disgusted by her.

"Of course not," she said stiffly, blinking away the dazzling stars which had popped into her eyes the moment Luke had started kissing her. "No. Definitely not."

Oh, how could she have been so foolish?

Mortification was in her very bones, though Peggy wasn't entirely sure whether it was that or lust. Perhaps both.

Because she had wanted him. Though she knew it was most uncouth for a lady to even consider a dalliance of any sort, she had wanted him. Wanted to complete what it was they had started a year ago. Wanted to know what it was to kiss and be kissed, hold and be held. To know a man so utterly, one could hardly walk afterward.

Not that she was thinking of that!

But it seemed now that her declaration of love was insufficient. Or her person was lacking. Or her kissing was inadequate.

Whatever it was, Peggy never wanted to be reminded of the evening she had thrown herself at Luke Beauchamp, Duke of Ashcott . . . only to be rejected.

With shaking hands, she smoothed her skirts. "R-Right. Well, I'll bid you goodnight."

Luke was staring at her with something akin to disappointment.

Him, disappointed? What, did he think she was made of stone? No, she was flesh and blood. It was only natural what she craved, was it not?

"That's a shame," said Luke heavily.

Peggy had taken just a step away. Every inch felt like torture, yet he had spoken as though she were the one inflicting this separation on them, not him.

She had invited him up to her bedchamber. Could she have been any more plain?

"That's a *shame?*" Peggy repeated, heat flooding her core, pooling between her legs in a most irritatingly distracting way. "It was *your* decision."

"Decision?" Luke was staring as though she had started speaking Mandarin.

She nodded, hoping to goodness no one would notice her go upstairs to her guest bedchamber. Her face must be almost beetroot! Not surprising, after all that kissing.

"Yes, decision," Peggy said, resenting the embarrassment she felt. *Was he really going to make her say it?* "I told you I loved you, kissed you, then invited you upstairs to my bedchamber. And you—"

Luke groaned, dropping his head into his hands. "Oh God, that was a close one."

Peggy stared. *A close one? What on earth was he talking about?*

Then suddenly she had been pulled into his embrace and Luke's arms were around her, holding her close. And though she could feel the hardness of his chest, and the hardness of something lower down, this was not a lustful embrace, but a . . . Peggy could hardly describe it. *Perhaps a loving one? Not that he had said anything about love.*

"Christ, what a misunderstanding, and to happen at such a time!" came Luke's voice from just behind her ear.

Peggy struggled to pull herself free. *Misunderstanding?*

"I was quite clear," she said, trying not to think how shameful this entire moment had become. "I asked you—"

"I thought you were suggesting that we should go upstairs," Luke said heavily, a weary smile on his face.

Peggy frowned. "I—"

"To separate bedchambers," Luke added. "That's what I thought you meant. That we were . . . well, getting carried away here, and we should stop."

Her mouth fell open. "Stop?"

Stop doing what was so intense, and pleasurable, and special? Stop kissing and being kissed? Stop the journey which they had started, full of teasing possibilities and hinted delights?

Understanding made her shoulders sag with relief. "You did not wish to stop kissing me?"

"Peggy Everleigh," said Luke softly, cupping her cheek and looking deep into her eyes. "There is not a moment in my life when I have ever wanted to stop kissing you."

Peggy smiled shyly, his words soaring through her, making it impossible to speak.

He wanted to keep kissing her—he loved her.

He must do. Oh, Luke hadn't said the words, but in a way he did not need to. Did she not know him better than anyone in the world? And this time at the Sedleys'—it had only increased her understanding of him. Luke was a man who had never been encouraged to speak his mind. In fact, he had been punished for it.

No wonder the scoundrel had found it almost impossible to speak last year. Why the last year had been so silent. Why these days had been so fractured as they had tried to dance around the fact that they loved each other.

Peggy lifted a hand to cover Luke's on her cheek. She wanted to feel him, luxuriate in every sensation he could give her. After all, it would not be long before they were wed. He had already asked her, and she had said yes. True, a few misunderstandings had got in their way since then. But all had been removed.

Joy surged through Peggy, a joy she knew that could never be removed. He was hers. Luke was the best thing that had ever happened to her.

Now she was going to enjoy him.

"So you want . . ." Peggy said, hardly knowing where her boldness was coming from. "You want to bed me?"

"I want to bed you, and make love to you, and worship you, and tease you so much you can barely speak," Luke said with a growl.

Peggy could do nothing but lean forward and kiss him eagerly. There had been a time when she would wait for him to kiss her, but no longer. She would take what she wanted.

And it appeared Luke was quite of the same mind. His kiss was dark, desperate, his mouth parting hers swiftly. Peggy moaned at the pleasure roaring through her as his tongue worshipped her mouth. He knew precisely what to do to make her quiver—knew what she wanted. How she wanted to be touched.

Oh, Luke . . .

"Peggy," Luke breathed.

Peggy blinked. Perhaps she had said that part aloud. Well, what did it matter? She could be open now.

"If this were my house I'd take you right here, right now," Luke said in a ragged voice.

Peggy flushed—partly at the lewd suggestion, and partly at how much it appealed. "We can't do that!"

"Not here," he agreed, one of his hands snaking down her arm to clasp her own. "No, I think in this case, stealing upstairs might be the best suggestion. I want you under me, Peggy. A bed will do just as well as a rug."

Peggy swallowed all her questions, her curiosity. She didn't have to ask. Within a few minutes, she would know.

"We . . . we'll have to be quiet," she said breathlessly. "The house is full of guests, if anyone were to hear—"

"You're right," Luke said with a wry smile. "Most definitely. Come on."

He pulled her forward and Peggy allowed him to do so. She'd follow this man anywhere.

But what she had not expected, when they had stepped out of the drawing room and into the corridor, was that he would take her left.

It was right to the staircase, wasn't it? She was always getting turned around in this place, but she was almost certain—

"Luke!" Peggy gasped.

It was impossible not to. He had just reached a side door that led outside onto the lawn, and without hesitation he had opened it. Opened it and pulled her outside.

"Luke, where are we—"

"You'll see," muttered Luke, glancing over his shoulder as he pulled her across the lawn. There was a wicked grin on his face she had seen only a few times before.

Every time, things had ended in mischief.

Excitement kept Peggy breathless as they did the unthinkable and crept along a gravel path. Anyone who looked out of the house would see—would suspect, surely, that something untoward was going on!

Yet this did not feel untoward. This felt most natural. As though she had been waiting her whole life to sneak through someone else's garden hand in hand with Luke.

Peggy's breath was short as Luke finally straightened up and halted.

"Here," he said simply.

Her eyes widened. *Surely not.* "You cannot be serious!"

It was the kitchen garden.

Moonlight streamed from the cloudless sky, lighting up the walled garden as though it were a midsummer day. Not a breeze moved. The trees stood, resplendent with fruit and leaves, and there was a strange sort of humming energy coming from the flower beds. As though the life sprouting within them was calling out to the world.

Peggy swallowed. *Make love outdoors?*

"No one will hear us here," said Luke quietly beside her. "I doubt anyone will disturb us. Not at this time. It's past midnight."

Past—past midnight? How long had they been conversing? And kissing? *Long enough, clearly.*

"I . . . I don't . . . you are certain we will not be disturbed?" Peggy asked softly.

Luke turned to her. There was such devotion on his face she almost gasped. "You think I would share this moment—or risk losing it? Peggy, you are everything to me. Up there, in that house? You're right. We'll be overheard."

Peggy swallowed again, her mouth unaccountably dry. "I can be quiet—"

"Not with what I have planned," Luke growled with a wolfish grin.

Oh, it was too much! Yet he was right, she could not disagree with his logic. Out here in the garden, half a mile from the house, no one would hear them. No one would see them.

They would be truly alone.

"Let me love you, Peggy," Luke breathed, a hand drifting to her waist, pulling her closer. "Let this be the first of many times I give you such hedonistic bliss, you can't remember your own name."

Peggy shivered. He had always been a temptation. The very moment she had seen him, she had known he could bring a woman to ecstasy.

Until now, she had always wondered whether she would be that woman.

"Love me, Luke," Peggy begged, taking in his heady scent, seeing his desire for her in his eyes. "Love me."

It appeared he did not need much of an invitation. With a strength that surprised even her, Luke lifted her off her feet, scooping her up in his arms as though she weighed nothing.

"Luke!"

"Let's find you a little lawn, shall we?" he said with a grin, striding along the kitchen garden gravel path toward the fruit trees.

Peggy could have guessed, the moment they entered the kitchen garden, that this would be where he'd want her. It was where they had almost kissed, where Luke had given her his apology, albeit in flower form.

Where something in them, between them, had changed. Forever.

The soft verge underneath the apple tree was filled with the aromatic scent of the fruit.

Peggy sighed as Luke laid her down beneath it, and lifted up a hand to welcome him down with her. "Luke, I—what do you think you're doing!"

It was impossible to restrain her surprise. Peggy stared as Luke knelt, not beside her as she had expected, but far lower down her body. By her knees, in fact.

And that was not all. Instead of seeking to remove her gown, as she had thought he would, the man seemed interested only in . . .

Well. Lifting her skirts.

"Trust me," said Luke with a grin. "You do trust me, don't you, Peggy?"

Peggy met his eyes.

Not in the slightest, she was tempted to say. *You're a rogue, a blackguard, a rake. The whole of Society knows you cannot be trusted, and so do I.*

And I wouldn't trust you for the rest of my life, if you'd let me.

"Yes."

Luke's grin widened. "Good. You be as loud as you like."

Peggy frowned at his words. *Loud? Why on earth would she be loud? There was no reason for—*

Then she knew precisely why.

"Luke," she moaned.

Now she knew why he had not immediately covered her body with his and kissed her passionately on the mouth. It was because Luke had other ideas—far better ideas, Peggy could not help thinking as she allowed her head to drop back, losing herself in the sensation.

The sensation of Luke's head underneath her skirts. His fingers pressing against her thighs, opening them up for him. His tongue, teasing out of his mouth and across her—

"Luke," whimpered Peggy, unable to stop herself.

The night was silent other than the sound of his passion and her moans. How could she stay silent, when such sensations were darting in and out of her secret place?

Oh, the warmth of his tongue, the way it seemed to know precisely what she wanted!

Peggy arched her back and thrust her hips forward, just slightly, before immediately ceasing. *What did she think she was doing, the harlot!*

But beneath her skirt came a gentle moan and, just for a moment, Luke ceased his licking. "God, I liked that. Do it again."

Peggy blinked up at the apple tree in wonder. "Do . . . do it again?"

But Luke did not reply. His tongue had entered her once more and Peggy could not help it. Her hips bucked, drawing him in, and she moaned as his hands gripped her hips, pulling her closer.

As though he wanted more of her. As though he was relishing this just as much as she was.

Giving herself up to the rippling feeling of decadence pouring through her body, Peggy allowed her head to tilt back and her eyes to close. Oh, this was wonderful, whatever this was building in her between her legs.

She bucked again and the sensations peaked. "Oh, God!"

Peggy's body took over as though it knew far better than she did what she wanted—what she needed. Almost astonished at the pleasure building within her, her hips wriggled and bucked as Luke's tongue built a rhythm that rose, rose, until—

"Luke, Luke, yes!"

She could not help it. The ecstasy was overwhelming, a pressure cascading through her that she had never expected, never known. And she could not be quiet as the waves of that pleasure strengthened rather than ebbed away. Peggy could see nothing but stars as she cried out with the sensuality of it.

Quiet? She could never be quiet with Luke doing that.

Eventually the waves subsided. Peggy blinked. The apple tree appeared before her. So did Luke's face.

"Good God, I could get used to that," he growled, pushing up her skirts to her waist.

Peggy merely stared, dazzled with the satisfaction he had given. "Y-You could?"

She had never thought a gentleman would wish to give such ecstasy as that. Unselfish, entirely focused on her, no thought for his own satisfaction at all.

Parts of her secret place were still quivering when Luke kissed the corner of her mouth. "I—damn it, Peg, I want all of you—"

"Then take me," Peggy said urgently, spreading her legs so

that he nestled between them. "Take me."

He wanted all of her? Did he not understand—could he not see he had all of her? That she was ruined now for all other men? Not because he had touched her, and kissed her, and licked her there and brought her to ecstasy. No, it was because she belonged to him. Peggy knew, without a shadow of a doubt, that she was his. His, to do what he wanted with.

Luke dipped his head to capture her lips, just for a moment. "There's no going back from this."

His passionate eyes met hers. Peggy knew he had to see, not just hear from her mouth, that she wanted him just as much as he wanted her. *Well, that was easily remedied.*

Reaching up, Peggy took hold of his shirt and ripped it open. Buttons flew everywhere and she was rewarded with the sight of dark hair trailing toward—

Breeches. Open.

Peggy's eyes widened. "Oh, my."

Well, it wasn't as though she didn't know what lovemaking was, in theory.

"You are not afraid?"

Peggy saw his care for her, his devotion. If she asked him to stop, even at this point, with her skirts at her waist and his manhood pressed against her hip, he would stop.

"I think we've talked enough," Peggy said with what she hoped was a bold and endearing smile. "Love me, Luke. Love me like you wanted to when you first met me."

Luke breathed a laugh as he nuzzled her neck, his hand moving to guide his manhood. "How did you know?"

"I've always known," gasped Peggy, arching her back as he slowly entered her. Inch by inch, she shifted to accommodate him. "I could see it in your eyes at Almack's. You wanted to push me up against a pillar and rut with me."

Luke moaned and she reveled in the way her words had such power over him. "I did."

"And I wanted you to," muttered Peggy, hardly knowing

how she had such bravery to admit this. After all this time, the truth seemed strange to finally speak. "If you'd taken me then, that very night, I would have let you."

They were both breathing heavily. Peggy adored the way she could feel Luke inside her, every breath reminding her that, finally, they were one.

"Good God, Peggy, you're better than anything I could have imagined," Luke said, kissing her fiercely as he almost pulled out of her then plunged into her once more.

Peggy whimpered, clutching his shoulders. The movement had been slight, yet it had sparked pleasure through her—a pleasure she now knew and wanted again.

"You'll never have to do without me again," she whispered as Luke once again built the rhythm his body seemed to have been made for.

"You're the best thing I've known, Peggy," Luke said, voice ragged. "The best thing."

Peggy arched her back, thrusting her hips upward to meet his own, and the force of the intensity almost pushed her over the edge. Nothing could ever compare to this.

"The best thing in life," she whimpered, now holding onto his shoulders for dear life, "is a duke—oh, yes!"

The second time she climaxed was somehow more powerful than the first. As Peggy cried out, Luke suddenly thrust into her hard, not once, not twice, but thrice, exhaling her name.

"Peggy, Peggy!"

And then he collapsed into her arms.

Peggy held him. Her heart was thundering, matched by the pace of Luke's own. She could feel it through his chest. At last, they had found their way back to each other.

This was the beginning of the rest of their lives.

CHAPTER FIFTEEN

28 August, 1811

I T WAS ALL Luke could do the next morning to keep a straight face as he entered the breakfast room and saw there was only one seat available.

It had to be a sign.

"Ah, Ashcott, we were beginning to wonder what had happened to you!" said Sedley with a smile at the head of the table. "About to send out a search party, weren't we, Braedon?"

"Most unaccountable absence, I thought," said the Viscount Braedon with what he evidently thought was a roguish wink. "It's not as though this is the sort of house party where guests start bed hopp—"

"Do sit down, Your Grace," interrupted the Duchess of Sedley with a calm voice but pink cheeks. "More *tea*, Lord Braedon?"

It was elegantly done. Luke had to admit, as he stepped around the table to the only empty seat, the duchess had managed to stop Braedon in his tracks more than once during his visit. If he were any judge, the viscount would not be receiving another invitation.

But he couldn't think about that now. Not as he pulled out

the chair beside Peggy and sat beside her. Just inches from her.

Her sleeve brushed up against his own.

"Damned rude of you, if you ask me," came a rather bad-tempered voice. "Keeping us all waiting. Not gentlemanly at all."

Luke looked across Peggy with a smile for the gentleman on her other side.

Lord Castor was glaring, face red and expression dogged.

"Why, Castor, I did not think I asked you," said Luke softly, so only the three of them could hear him. "Yes, tea would be most pleasant, I thank you."

The idiot was prevented from replying by the footman who leaned between Luke and Peggy to pour tea. It was a relief, really. It gave him the opportunity to gather himself.

You have won, Luke told himself, and he took a deep breath.

And he had won. Oh, not that it was a fair fight, really. He almost felt sad for the poor fellow. Peggy had been his for a long time. Long before Castor had ever met her.

"And how did you sleep, Lady Margaret?" Luke asked amiably as the footman returned to his station by the wall.

It was the wrong thing to say. His beloved's cheeks became a pink he had not intended as she murmured something indistinct in response—but then they had agreed, hadn't they?

"We will just have to pretend our friendship—"

Luke had snorted as they had lain there, Peggy in his arms, underneath the apple tree. "Friendship, indeed!"

A relatively gentle finger poked his side. "Our friendship, I say, is improving. That's all."

"You think I can just sit there at the breakfast table tomorrow, pretending this hasn't happened?" Luke had asked incredulously.

It had seemed impossible. Be in the presence of Peggy and not stare as though she were the only thing worth looking at? Be around her and not wish to be constantly pressing his lips to the back of her hand? Or her palm. Or her shoulder, the little crest of her collarbone just aching to be—

"It's the only way," Peggy had whispered, moonlight scattering through the leaves above them. "For now. Until I speak to my brother."

Luke's stomach had lurched then and it lurched now at the breakfast table at the mere memory of her words.

Yes. Her brother. Henry Everleigh, Duke of Dulverton.

It was probably best he did not hear tittle-tattle about how his sister and the man who had jilted her, in Dulverton's eyes, were attached once more.

Still, it was a challenge to sit beside Peggy and pretend he was not conscious of her every movement. The way she tilted her teacup, bringing it to her exquisite lips. The way she stoically ate the disgusting eggs the Duchess of Sedley preferred without complaint. The way she—

"I said, did you sleep poorly last night?" repeated the older Mr. Marnion from across the table.

Luke started. "I beg your pardon?"

It was an innocent enough question, he supposed, but he still took a moment to be sure his face was sufficiently calm. If he wasn't careful, someone was going to guess. Luke did everything he could not to glance at Peggy to his right, but it was difficult. In his peripheral vision, he could see a wry smile curling her lips.

"Did you sleep ill? Last night. Is that why you were so late down?" persisted Mr. Marnion.

Well, yes. He supposed that was true.

"I slept very little indeed," said Luke brightly, still trying not to look at her. *Damn this temptation.* "In fact, I would hazard to say I have never slept so little in all my—"

"Oh, what a cough you have there, Lady Margaret," said Miss Yates calmly. "Honey in your tea, perhaps?"

"I think that would be appropriate," said Peggy quietly, her cheeks burning. "Thank you, Miss Yates."

Luke hid a smile as he took a few mouthfuls of the bacon and sausage which had been placed upon his plate by a footman.

Well, he hadn't said anything too outrageous. Not unless one knew the precise reason for that lack of sleep.

"Don't worry," came a whisper Luke could just hear under the genteel hubbub of table conversation. "See? No one's noticed."

Glancing up, he saw a footman remove a laden plate from before the duchess as she leaned back from her husband, the whispering over.

He suppressed another smile. The duchess thought that no one had noticed that, for the third morning in a row, she had not eaten anything for breakfast? She could not be more incorrect. Not that he was going to point it out. He wasn't the sort of fool who revealed other people's secrets. No matter how tempting it was.

A gentle movement beside him. Peggy leaned past him to pick up the salt, and as she did so she breathed, "When do you think they'll announce it?"

She was clever, this Peggy of his. So intelligent. So observant.

"I suppose when the quickening happens," he said to his teacup as he pretended to take a sip. "I certainly wouldn't announce anything until then."

He shouldn't have spoken so openly. When Luke put his teacup down, it was to see Peggy's cheeks delicately pink.

"You . . . you have thought about it, then?"

Luke's stomach turned over. And he couldn't blame the Duchess of Sedley's eggs for he'd had none.

Yes, he wanted to say. *Yes, every moment since I have known I was in love with you. From the moment I knew I had to offer for your hand, absent brother be damned. What man wouldn't consider the children we could make together, the life that could spark within you, that I put there?*

"Yes," he said quietly.

It was as though he had shouted it. The already pink spots on Peggy's cheeks darkened most delightfully, and she swiftly looked at her plate.

That would be a conversation they would have later, Luke

thought. One of many. There was so much they had to discuss, so much he wanted to plan.

Though of course, there were a few things to be sorted out first.

"Let me help you to more breakfast, Lady Margaret," Castor was saying on her other side. "You've barely touched your food—a fried tomato, perhaps? Some mushrooms?"

It rather astonished Luke that he was able to look upon the scene with equanimity. Just a day ago, he would have been raging that the idiot was acting so devoted to the woman he loved. The woman he knew, even if Peggy had not admitted it then, belonged to him.

But as he watched Peggy demur and say she was perfectly replete, thank you, Luke found he had nothing but pity for the man. He knew what it was to look upon a woman and not have her. It wasn't Castor's fault he had chosen to pursue a woman who was already spoken for. He hadn't known that.

And Peggy was most alluring.

It was all Luke could do to concentrate on his own breakfast. Spending the rest of the Sedley house party pretending they were nothing to each other—how on earth would he manage it?

"What are everyone's plans for today?" Mrs. Marnion was asking further up the table. "If it is not quite so hot, I thought I might take a turn around the garden."

"I would do so swiftly, for the heat threatens just as much as it did yesterday," said Miss Yates blithely.

"I would accompany you, but M-Miss Yates and I have agreed to go on a short ride," piped up the younger Mr. Marnion.

Luke grinned and threw the boy a wink. The young man flushed.

"N-Nothing of that nature, I can assure you," he hissed back.

Grinning, Luke inclined his head. "Of course."

"There's only room for so much mischief in this place," came Peggy's quiet words beside him. "How much do you think the house can hold?"

A thrill sparked up Luke's spine. "It doesn't matter to me. I always take my passion outside, if I can help it."

There it was—the sudden intake of breath, the brush of her hand against his. Just slight. No one would notice, Luke was sure. No one except him. His whole body was roaring with delight at the quiet flirtation.

They had missed out on so much. Lost so much time, just because of his own stupidity and inability to recognize how desperately Peggy had wanted him to stay, to come back and face her brother.

But they could make up for that now. They had all the time in the world.

"Would you like to go for a walk, Lady Margaret?" came the eager voice of Castor.

Once again, Luke expected jealous rage but found only calm and a little pity in response to the viscount's suggestion.

"Oh, no, thank you," she said gently. "I think I will spend the morning and early afternoon in the drawing room. It is most warm, and those are the coolest parts of the house."

"I thought you enjoyed being warm." Castor dropped his voice as Mrs. Marnion's conversation continued, advising the others on the best route for a ride. "That was my impression, anyway."

Luke stiffened.

Well, really! Was that any way to talk to a lady, let alone Peggy?

But it appeared Peggy was more than calm enough to respond, and with a most ladylike answer. "I enjoy heat in its place, Lord Castor. But not indiscriminately."

He wanted to stand up and cheer, to proclaim that she was the most remarkable woman he had ever met!

Thankfully, Luke managed to contain himself. He could not, however, prevent himself from glancing over at the man to see how he had taken Peggy's slight reproof.

For some reason, Castor was smiling. "Of course, Lady Margaret. You must say that."

Luke tried not to roll his eyes, but it was hard work. The man was an absolute idiot—but it wouldn't be long until the truth was out. Then Castor would have to go back to the drawing board. Why not chase after Miss Yates? She surely wouldn't be taken in by that youth Marnion.

Still the anger he had expected to rise did not flourish. He had won. Not over Castor, but for Peggy's heart—and that was far more important.

Just as Luke was about to say something to Peggy—precisely what, he did not know—there was a gasp from the head of the table.

He jerked his head to Sedley. "News?"

It could only be ill news, the way the man had sounded. Luke had half expected his host to be clutching a letter in his hand. Instead he saw a newspaper, half folded and now dropped onto the duke's plate. The disgusting egg crackled underneath it.

"What is it?" asked Sedley's wife quickly.

Luke's stomach lurched to see her concern. Soon, Peggy could do that in public without fear of her brother discovering their renewed affections.

"It's Chetnole," Sedley was saying quietly. "Word's come back from France and he's—"

"Not dead?" The Duchess of Sedley clutched her chest. "Oh, Byron, how awful—"

"No, it's not that. At least, I don't think so," said Sedley heavily.

The conversation had now caught the attention of the entire room, and Luke wasn't surprised. France could feel like a long way away sometimes—in the stickiness of Almack's, in the thrill of the hunt, in the arms of a beautiful woman. But he had been there long enough to know his time there would never truly leave him. Being a veteran of that struggle, even though he had picked up secrets rather than swords, was not something he would ever forget.

There was that same sort of tension now in the room. Luke

could feel it.

His instinct was to take Peggy out of the breakfast room under some pretense—a lost book, perhaps, or a request to see the embroidery she was working on. Anything to ensure she did not hear the terrible details of that place.

But Sedley sighed, and Luke recalled that the duke would never be so crass as to say something awful before the ladies.

Still. What he did say was hardly an improvement.

"He's missing," Sedley said dully. "Chetnole. Missing. I never would have thought it."

Luke's pulse halted, then restarted. *Missing.* However Sedley might frame it, it could only be bad news eventually. One did not go missing in France only to be found later.

No, wait—he had heard of it, once. Didn't Sedley's brother-in-law, the duchess's brother . . .?

No, he could not be remembering that correctly.

The duchess placed a hand on her husband's arm. "All hope is not lost. Beth proved that."

Beth? Who on earth was Beth?

But it appeared Luke was not going to find out. The conversation had moved on—at least, as far as it could with Braedon in the room, God help them all.

"Goodness, how dreadful!" Braedon said with a cheerful sigh. "I would hate to go out there to France. It all sounds so dangerous."

"Sometimes it's the best way to serve one's country," Mr. Marnion said stiffly.

Luke remembered, all too late, that the Marnion family had lost a son to the war against Napoleon. *Oh dear.*

It appeared Braedon was only just recalling too, for his face had gone scarlet and his fingers were twisting together before his plate. "Ah . . . ah. Yes. Very impressive, of course—"

"I am sorry for the news of your friend, Your Graces. We shall have to pray he is found," Miss Yates said smoothly. "An honorable profession. Don't you agree, Lord Braedon?"

"Yes—yes, I most certainly do," said Braedon gratefully while Luke snorted. "Most definitely. In fact—"

Luke did not concentrate on the viscount's desperate attempt to dig himself out of the hole he had created. He was far more interested in their hosts.

Sedley looked awful. His face was pale, and he looked morosely at his wife.

Chetnole. Luke was sure he had spoken to him once in the Dulverton Club. Before he had left for France himself, naturally. The moment Peggy's brother had discovered him in his drawing room, there was no possibility of returning there.

Chetnole. Well, he would have to keep an ear to the ground when he returned to London, Luke thought pensively. If there was any chance they had contacts in common, perhaps he could be of some service.

"—losing someone like that—missing, with no knowledge of whether he will be found," Lord Castor was saying to Miss Yates. "Heaven forbid . . ."

Luke started.

Not because of the man's words. It was the same genteel pattering one would expect after such news.

No, it was because there was something on his knee.

He glanced down. Peggy had surreptitiously placed her hand on his knee under the table, away from the prying eyes of the other guests.

In almost any other situation, her movement would have been deeply sensual. Suggestive, even, that she wished them to find a deserted bit of garden and put it to good use. But there was something different in the way she did it. Luke could not explain how her unspoken feelings were so clear to him, but they were. She was comforting him.

Peggy knew he had been in France. Though he had been careful not to give any details, she understood the disquiet he felt from hearing that this Chetnole was missing.

He was so fortunate to have found her—again. Now all he

had to do was make what they had shared yesterday into something much more permanent.

"I am leaving," Luke said.

It was only in the stunned silence, broken only by the sound of cutlery being placed back onto a plate, that he realized he had spoken aloud.

Ah. He had intended to say quietly to Peggy—but perhaps it was best this way. The whole party needed to know, after all.

"Leaving?" said Miss Yates blankly. "Now?"

"This morning, yes, if I can get my valet in order," said Luke cheerfully.

Yes, it was best to do it now—then it would be all sorted before the end of the week.

"Goodness," said Castor with an unbelievable sigh. "We will miss you."

It was on the tip of Luke's tongue to say he absolutely wouldn't, but he managed to restrain himself. No need to kick a man when he was down. Even if he didn't know he was down.

"You are?" Peggy said quietly.

Luke's manhood stirred, but so did his affection, his desire to protect and care for her. She was so precious to him, and he had to prove that to her. Beyond any doubt.

He may not have told her he loved her, not precisely, but he had tried to with the flowers. And what he was about to do would show her—as well as tell her—that his devotion and affection was absolute.

"Trust me," he breathed so no one else could hear.

For some reason, there was fear in Peggy's eyes as she swallowed and nodded without saying a word.

Fear? It made no sense—but then, Luke did not have the time to explain now. The idea had floated into his mind, already formed, and he was itching to carry it out.

"I'll be gone before luncheon," he said aloud. "Yes. Yes, it's time to leave."

CHAPTER SIXTEEN

29 August, 1811

PEGGY STABBED VICIOUSLY at the embroidery she was working on.

It was surely better to get all her anger out on the fabric and thread, than on a certain someone who had decided to abandon her once again.

"I am leaving."

"You are?"

"I'll be gone before luncheon. Yes. Yes, it's time to leave."

It was infuriating!

The blue thread she had chosen in Bath for the swallow on the embroidery pattern she had selected was a beautiful blue. The same blue as Luke's eyes when he had professed his love. Again.

"Carnations, of course."

"For . . .?"

"L-Love. Like roses, but more creative."

Peggy stabbed once again through the fabric, delighted to feel the tension splintering from her shoulders as she did so.

"Goodness," said Lord Braedon with a laugh. "What did that fabric ever do to you?"

Peggy looked up with a glare before remembering herself.

She was seated in the drawing room, the calmest and usually coolest part of the house. And she was not alone.

Lord Braedon was reading a newspaper, though clearly he did not find its contents that interesting, or he would not have been watching her. Miss Yates was similarly occupied with embroidery, though she was managing to do so without as much ire. And the young Mr. Marnion was shooting Miss Yates such longing looks, Peggy was almost startled to have seen them.

It appeared Miss Yates had two gentlemen to choose from: young Mr. Marnion and Lord Castor.

Go for the man without the title, Peggy wanted to say, though of course she was not nearly intimately acquainted with the woman to speak so openly. *A title can only get you so far. Devotion as I have just seen on Mr. Marnion's face, however—that would last a lifetime.*

Should last a lifetime. Peggy tried to push the thought from her mind, but it was difficult to do after such a tumultuous few days.

After everything they had been through last year—after falling in love, promising themselves to each other, breaking that connection, going without hearing anything from him for months, then arguing fit to burst countless times here at the Sedleys' . . .

And that kiss. The kitchen garden. The realization, just a couple nights ago, that they could not live without each other. Sharing the most intimate, the most special of connections.

And now he was gone.

A lifetime indeed, thought Peggy darkly. It didn't seem possible to keep that man still for five minutes together. And Luke was apparently in love with her!

Not in love enough to stay, whispered a cruel voice in the back of her mind. Try as she might, it was difficult to completely ignore the thought.

Because wasn't it true? After she had given herself to him— willingly, of course—and shared such passion, why would Luke just disappear like that? What could possibly be so important that he would just leave?

And why hadn't he said when he was coming back?

"Sometimes you truly have to push the needle through with a significant effort," Miss Yates was saying to Lord Braedon, as though his words required a response. "You should try it sometime, my lord. You may find it entertains more than your newspaper."

Peggy would have smiled if such sadness had not been overwhelming other feelings.

That night . . . it had been everything to her. Luke, the man she loved. Their final understanding had been so sweet, at least in her eyes.

But what if it hadn't been for him? What if—what if this entire thing had just been a completion of what he had started last year? What if that had been Luke's intention all along? To bed her, not wed her?

Her stomach twisted uncomfortably. Peggy tried to shuffle slightly on the sofa but it did nothing to alleviate her anxiety.

Surely he could not have abandoned her again?

"—such a shame that old Ashcott is gone."

His name caught her interest and despite herself, Peggy looked up.

Lord Braedon was now—there was only one word for it— lounging. He was leaning back in his armchair with such comfort and presence, Peggy was not surprised Miss Yates raised an eyebrow. It was all very well to loll about like that in your own home—but in the home of another?

"I suppose he will be back soon," Miss Yates said quietly.

Peggy's lungs constricted. What did Miss Yates know that she herself did not? Was it possible—surely it was not possible Luke had told Miss Yates when he was returning, and not her?

"I don't know, he did not mention any particular return date to me," said Lord Braedon lazily. "I rather got the impression, in fact, that he wasn't intending to come back."

"Ouch!"

Peggy's cheeks flushed as the eyes of the room turned to her.

"Lady Margaret, are you quite well?" asked Miss Yates politely.

Trying to smile through the pain, Peggy nodded. "Just—just nicked my thumb with my needle, that's all."

It was actually quite a painful injury, though it was small.

Lord Braedon shook his head with a tut. "I did think you were stabbing it a little too forcefully."

Peggy did her best not to shoot daggers at the irritating man. Did he have to be so inquisitive, so invested in everyone's business? Must he lecture her on the proper way to embroider, as though he had any idea what she was doing?

Try as she might, it was becoming impossible to merely ignore the man's inane smile. She would have to say something, Lord help her.

"Actually, Lord Braedon—" Peggy began icily.

"Lord Braedon." The young Mr. Marnion had risen to his feet, cheeks pink, but face determined. "Would you be so good as to show me the gun you'll be borrowing from the Duke of Sedley tomorrow for the hunt? I believe it is in the gun room."

He spread out his hand toward the door.

It was well done. Appealing to the older man's expertise and getting him out of harm's way at the same time. Perhaps the young Mr. Marnion had a bright future in Society after all. Despite his mother.

Lord Braedon rose with enthusiasm. "Always happy to teach a youngster the ropes! Now, you'll notice that there are a great many different kinds of . . ."

His voice faded away as the two gentlemen left the drawing room.

Peggy sighed with relief. At least she could now be left alone in quiet. The last thing she wanted to do was converse—

"I thought you were going to stab him in the eye with that needle," Miss Yates said nonchalantly. "Not that he wouldn't deserve it. But still."

A laugh, dry and bitter, escaped Peggy. "You know, I wouldn't have discounted it if Mr. Marnion hadn't rescued him," she admitted.

It was a strange admission to make to a relative stranger. Now she came to think about it, she hardly knew anything about Miss Yates, save that the Sedleys considered her a suitable guest.

She probably shouldn't be telling her she had seriously considered stabbing a viscount.

"But I wouldn't actually have done it," added Peggy with a smile. "Obviously."

"Obviously," said Miss Yates with a bland smile. "Not with an embroidery needle. I find pins are far better suited for such a thing."

She dipped her head back to her own embroidery.

Pins, indeed! What on earth was the woman on about? She was joking. Yes, she was joking, Peggy tried to reassure herself as she ignored the stinging sensation in her thumb and focused instead on her embroidery.

A small red stain covered part of the cloth. *Oh, bother.*

"But if you'll take my advice," said Miss Yates calmly, as though she had not been momentarily advising a lady to attack a man, "you'll ignore Lord Braedon. He's harmless."

Peggy forced herself to smile. "I-I know. I wasn't actually going to—"

"There are far more dangerous men here at the Sedleys'," Miss Yates continued, as though Peggy had not spoken. "You would do well to avoid *him*, if you take my drift."

Her calculating eyes met Peggy's and she shivered.

More dangerous men?

It was quite a claim. If Peggy's mind had not already been whirling with the loss of Luke so swiftly after they had finally reconciled, she would probably have had the presence of mind to inquire just who Miss Yates was referring to.

Although of course, there could be no doubt.

Peggy sighed. It was his father's fault, of course. Now that

Luke had admitted as much, it all made sense.

A father who demanded such coldness, such rigidness from his son was going to create a man who was just that. No wonder Luke had gained such a poor reputation in Society. Rake, scoundrel, rascal—it was just a misunderstanding of his character. And she knew that now, understood it in a way she never had before. The Luke who was opening up to her, who had been so vulnerable the last few days—no one else had seen that.

No, that particular Luke was all hers.

"I thank you," Peggy said formally after a moment's thought, "for your warning."

Not that it is necessary, she wanted to say but managed to stop herself as she watched Miss Yates continue with her embroidery. *Luke would never hurt me—not intentionally.*

Would he suddenly disappear after the cataclysmic discovery of their own mutual affection, without a single word as to where he was going or when he would be back?

Tension sparked across her shoulder blades, making her shiver.

Well, yes. But that wasn't on purpose, was it? He was coming back, wasn't he?

"I pray you heed it," said Miss Yates conversationally, as though they were discussing the weather. "A man like that is dangerous indeed, and you are altogether too close to him, Lady Margaret. If you do not mind me saying so."

Peggy's irritation flared. "Actually, I—"

"I only say this for your own good," said Miss Yates, speaking over her with a taut smile. "I promised your brother as much."

And only then did realization dawn.

Of course. Of course her brother did not entirely trust her to go into the country and forget about Luke—and quite rightly, too, as it turned out! She hadn't been able to forget Luke at all. But it was most galling indeed for Henry to have been proven right—and from afar. Through a proxy, no less!

Miss Yates. A spy for her brother.

"I did not realize you took such an interest in my affairs," Peggy said stiffly as a reproof.

Miss Yates evidently did not take it so. She smiled, and inclined her head. "Only when required, Lady Margaret."

Peggy put the embroidery on the sofa beside her. No, she'd had enough of this. She'd spent months moping about for Luke Beauchamp, finally decided she could no longer suffer by being in love, then been forced to confront her feelings yet again—then the brute had just up and left! And now her brother, the one man she had thought she could trust, was setting spies on her!

Embroidery was insufficient to forget the deeds of such miscreants. She needed a book.

"Good morning, Miss Yates," Peggy said politely as she left the drawing room.

"Lady Margaret," came the polite response of the woman she was leaving behind.

She would have to ask the Duchess of Sedley about her, Peggy decided. Stabbing eyes, pins over needles? It was all very strange. Probably not a suitable sort of companion for a duchess, after all.

The library was mercifully empty when she arrived, but it did not become the immediate sanctuary that she had hoped for. The instant she stepped inside, Peggy was visited by memories of the two encounters she and Luke had shared there.

"Well, if you won't do the gentlemanly thing and go away, I suppose I shall I have to leave. The outrage! Forced from a library!"

"If I can't have you for a wife, then can we at least be friends?"

Repressed desire shivered up Peggy's spine. Perhaps she had been too incautious. Too easily won. Perhaps Luke had thought her too eager to lift her skirts for him and had become repulsed. Perhaps—

"Ah, there you are," came a man's voice from behind her.

Her heart permitted her only a half an instant of happiness. It was a man's voice, true, and it could have been Luke's. But it wasn't.

Peggy turned to smile wearily at Lord Castor. *Could she not be given a moment's peace?*

"I've been looking for you everywhere," said Lord Castor cheerfully, stepping into the library and closing the door behind him. "I thought I might find you in here."

Her smile wavered. It was a lie, obviously. He hadn't searched the drawing room, where until a few minutes ago, the majority of the houseguests had been. But it was of no matter. It was a mere pleasantry, and Peggy had learned long ago that most of them were lies anyway. Dull, convenient lies.

"Well, I'm here," she said, trying to look just as pleased to see the viscount as he was to see her. "Just choosing a book. To read. Quietly."

Her gentle hint wasn't that gentle, but Peggy could see it was swiftly ignored anyway.

"Oh, the Sedleys have a great number of excellent tomes you can lose yourself in," said Lord Castor, stepping forward to a bookcase. "Here, let me recommend one."

Peggy's hopes sank as she stepped over to the shelf where the viscount was looking. She would merely have to be polite for a few minutes, that was all. Then she could take her book and— would it be considered rude if she took it up to her bedchamber? Could she claim a headache?

"You are an avid reader, I suppose," Lord Castor said with what he seemed to think was a charming smile.

Peggy tried to return the smile as she lifted a hand up to brush along the spines of the books. "I suppose—Castor!"

She had not intended to speak his name so informally, but she had little chance to say anything more.

In the flash of an eye, before she could do anything to stop him, Lord Castor had grabbed both her shoulders, pushed her against the bookcase, and brought his chest to press right against hers.

It was astoundingly uncomfortable. Peggy's hands lifted instinctively to press against his shoulders, attempting to free herself.

"Lord Castor, you forget yourself!" she cried.

Someone would hear—surely, someone would hear the commotion in here, and step into the library, and see . . .

Something that could be quickly misunderstood.

Peggy struggled against him, but Lord Castor was far stronger than he appeared. He kept her pinned against the bookcase, eyes lit up, his smile somehow joyless.

"Kiss me, Margaret," he breathed.

Peggy's eyes widened. "Certainly not!"

Her fingers were still pressed against his shoulders, but he showed no sign of budging.

"You would prefer to wait until after we are married?" Lord Castor said in an undertone. "Oh, Margaret, you are far too teasing—"

"After we—I beg your pardon!"

In her struggle to be free of the overenthusiastic viscount, her knee shifted—not by accident—and knocked solidly into the man's own leg. As Lord Castor stumbled back, reaching for his leg with a groan, Peggy hastily stepped away along the bookcase.

"You have forgotten yourself, and I suppose that is understandable, in a way," she said, not believing it. She needed to get out of the library. At once.

The trouble was, the instinct that had her step away from him also led her to take a step away from the door to the corridor, not toward it. She was near the window and would have to pass by the increasingly more irate man if she were to leave.

"Forgot myself? It is you who have forgotten yourself—it's me, Castor," said Lord Castor urgently, taking a step toward her. "Have you not encouraged me? Have you not been most impressed by my suit? Do not pretend that you have been unaware of my attentions!"

Peggy swallowed.

And this, her brother would surely say, was the problem when you used one man to distract from another.

She had never seriously considered Lord Castor as anything more than a conversational partner. Perhaps a dance partner, if the Sedleys had drawn up a set, but nothing more than that. Certainly not a marital partner!

Evidently she had not been quite as circumspect as she thought. Guilt twinged in Peggy's heart. She had never intended to wound Lord Castor, nor to mislead him in terms of her affections. It would be an awkward conversation, to be sure, but it would simply have to be so. Whether Luke was returning for her or not.

Pushing aside her final thought, Peggy said firmly, "Lord Castor. I am sorry if you have misunderstood—"

"Misunderstood? Margaret Everleigh, you have made it plain you wish to be my wife!"

"I have done absolutely no such thing," Peggy said swiftly, her chest tight.

There was a look on Lord Castor's face she did not like. A stern one. One that would brook no opposition.

"You . . . you mean to say you don't wish to marry me?" he said quietly.

There was a repressed sort of rage in his voice which caused fear to ripple up Peggy's spine. *He wouldn't do anything foolish, save declare his love for her,* she thought. *He was a viscount, and she the daughter and sister of a duke!*

"I have absolutely no wish to marry you," Peggy said decisively. "I regret it—the confusion," she added, upon seeing the look of astonishment on his face.

The astonishment, however, swiftly turned to something much darker.

"Well hell's bells, you have had me dancing along to your tune," Lord Castor spat. "Very clever of you. Well, I may not get what I want, Lady Margaret, but I'm sure as hell not leaving this room without something for my troubles."

And then it was happening again, all too swiftly, all too painfully—Lord Castor's hands on her elbows, holding her tight, and she was pressed against the bookcase and there was nowhere to go—

"Let go of me!" Peggy cried.

But there was no one to hear save Lord Castor, and he laughed as she struggled. "It'll be over all the sooner if you don't try to fight me off, Margaret, you'll see—"

"No," Peggy moaned, her voice hoarse, panic making any breath close to impossible.

His lips were coming closer and closer, and there was nothing she could do, no one to save her, she couldn't break free—

The library door crashed open.

# CHAPTER SEVENTEEN

"... I MAY NOT get what I want, Lady Margaret, but I'm sure as hell not leaving this room without something for my troubles."

It was the coldness of the voice that caught Luke's attention. He had minutes ago arrived back at the Sedleys', and had just finished a swift conversation with the duchess as to the best way to go about it.

Hell, he hardly knew what a woman wanted in this regard. And the duchess was happily married—very happily, if his suspicions about a new Sedley in the not-too-distant future were correct. Luke was certain the duchess could give him pointers on how such a speech should be made.

And so he was walking along the corridor past the library when he heard something most strange. A low voice. A voice full of menace and cruelty. And danger.

Were they playing charades in there?

"Let go of me!" a voice cried.

Luke froze, just a few steps passed the library.

That was no charade—no one could act that well. At least, no one here at the Sedleys' house party. And worse, that sounded like—

"It'll be over all the sooner if you don't try to fight me off, Margaret, you'll see—"

"No!"

Luke went cold.

That was Castor's voice—that cruel, nastiness he had thought he had seen once or twice coming to the foreground.

And the woman whose piteous moan had echoed around the library, just escaping under the door—the woman who was evidently in the idiot's clutches, desperate to escape . . .

Peggy.

Luke did not think. Thinking would take time and there was no time, he was sure of that.

Peggy needed him. There may have been several times she had needed him in the last year and he had not been there. Damn it all, he didn't even know about them. Had never bothered to ask.

But right now, she needed him and he was here. There was no second thought in his mind.

Lurching forward and wrenching open the door, Luke stepped into the library to see—

A nightmare.

There was Castor. His jacket was unbuttoned. That may have been for an entirely innocent reason, such as the day's soaring temperature. Young Mr. Marnion had taken to going around without his buttons done up, and no one would consider him a miscreant.

But it was worse than just that. Castor's face was red, his hands almost bone white. Because they were gripping the arms of Peggy Everleigh.

Peggy was crying.

Crying. He had made her cry—the blackguard had made his Peggy cry.

"Get your bloody hands off her!" Luke thundered with blinding rage, launching forward.

He had intended to wrench the rake off the sobbing woman, but Castor released Peggy the moment Luke approached.

"All a misunderstanding," Castor said swiftly, straightening his jacket and putting his hands up in mock surrender. "Complete confusion, I'd—"

"You shut your mouth or I'll shut it for you," Luke snapped, not turning to follow his movement.

He was far more interested in Peggy.

His heart sank then broke into a million pieces as he beheld her. Half the pins had come out of her hair which was mussed. Tears streaked down her face. Her fingers looked pained, as though she had attempted to fight him off.

Just for a moment, Luke closed his eyes and took a deep breath.

He had to control himself. Peggy needed him. He could not lose himself in pain and regret and thoughts of vengeance.

The old Luke, the one who had stormed out of the Dulverton house merely because he was piqued and had never returned? That Luke would have turned from Peggy, his uppermost thoughts focused solely on revenge. He would have demanded a duel from the sniveling Castor and shot him for good measure.

In short, he would have entirely lost sight of who was truly important in that room.

Luke opened his eyes as his pulse started, thankfully, to slow.

He had to ensure Peggy was—well, safe was not quite the right word. She had suffered something outrageous, something no woman, no person ever should.

Thank God he had been here in time.

Luke pushed the thought away to be examined another time. He could not allow the fear of what could have been to overwhelm him.

"Peg," he said softly.

Peggy would not meet his eye. She was staring at his cravat and seemed to be attempting to keep more tears falling.

Oh, Christ.

"Come on, Peggy," Luke said gently.

He had been about to care for her as she deserved, no thought for anyone else.

Fortunately for him, he saw the glint of the blade out of the corner of his eye.

"Luke!" screamed Peggy.

Her panic did not distract him. Taking a hurried step to the left and twirling around to face his cowardly attacker, Luke glared at the viscount who plainly thought he had nothing left to lose.

"She's mine!" Castor yelled, swinging the knife which had appeared from nowhere. "You found her with me, and you know what that means!"

Luke stepped back from the shimmering blade and tried to think as anger rose.

Yes, he did know what that meant. In most cases, a gentleman and a lady discovered in such a scandalous position would be forced, either by a father or brother, or merely by Society's expectations, to meet at the top of an aisle and make vows to each other.

The very thought was repellent. *Peggy, have to marry that wart? Marry the man who had clearly demanded a kiss and perhaps attempted even more?*

Over his dead body.

"You think you can take her from me, but you're wrong!" panted Castor, lunging with the blade.

Luke swiftly sidestepped him and brought both hands down, hard, on the man's wrist.

"Arrgh!"

The sudden jolting pain he had surely inflicted did precisely what Luke had intended. Castor's hand dropped the knife, his fingers flexing in agony.

"You blackguard!"

Luke ignored him. Though his breath was short and his mind was racing with what could have been—*waving a knife about, before a lady!*—he did what his instincts in France had taught him over the months he'd been there.

Swiftly leaning down and picking up the knife, he shoved it in his belt before glaring back up at the sniveling viscount.

"You, sir," Luke said darkly, wondering why on earth he was being so polite, "are a disgrace. You will leave the house of the Sedleys, who are good people—"

"There'll be a scandal!" Castor shot back, clutching his hands to his chest. "You know there will!"

Luke hesitated.

It was not an empty threat. He knew full well what Society could do to a woman's reputation. If even half of what Peggy had said was true, she had borne the brunt of the gossip after the news of their engagement—swiftly broken—slipped into the scandal sheets.

What would happen to Peggy now, after being embroiled in a second scandal? And with a man like Castor?

It was the dry, irritating laugh that followed the threat that made him do it. Luke knew he wasn't thinking clearly. Who could, after discovering such a scene? But it was Castor laughing, as though he had somehow won the high ground, that pushed Luke over the edge.

"I think you'll find that any lies you spread about my wife will be met with very severely, either by lawyer or by pistol," Luke said imperiously. "Mind you leave in the next ten minutes, Castor. I'll have Sedley throw you out in eleven."

"Your—your wife?"

Luke ignored the bastard's splutters. He didn't need to think about the blackguard anymore, did not care about him beyond the awareness that he was making his escape from the room as instructed. He had something—someone—far more important to consider.

He thought, for a moment, she was going to shy from him like a frightened horse as he approached. But Peggy merely stood still as he swept her up into his arms and pulled her close into his chest. Toward his heart.

Could she feel his heart, Luke wondered. *Did she know it beat only for her?*

"What on earth is going on?" asked a voice just outside the

library. "Who is—oh, my word. Ashcott."

Luke held his head up high as he carried Peggy out of the library to see not only the Duchess of Sedley, but Miss Yates and the young Mr. Marnion outside.

Peggy lowered her head, her hair falling past her face.

He had to protect her. Every instinct in his body was now centered on the delicate woman in his arms who had borne so much, and without the support of a soul.

Luke swallowed. "Lady Margaret is unwell."

"My goodness, right," said the duchess, her voice strengthening. "A doctor. I'll have Walsingham called. He's the absolute best. I needed to see him anyway, actually, ahem. No particular reason, I just—"

"A bath," Luke said with authority as he started to walk past the staring houseguests.

Did young Marnion have to make it so obvious he was goggling?

"I'll speak to one of the maids," said Miss Yates quietly. At least someone was keeping their head. "It'll be done in a jiffy—"

"—never a bad idea to see a doctor, even if there is no particular reason you need—"

Luke did not wait for the duchess to finish speaking. Peggy was now clutching him, her fingers tight around his cravat.

It was as though she were reaching into his very chest, terrified he would leave her. Leave her? He was never going to leave her presence again.

The distance from the library to Peggy's bedchamber was not overly far, but every step took an age, as far as Luke could tell. When he finally reached the bedchamber, there was already a frantic maid within it.

"Just a few more minutes, Y'Grace, m'lady, and I'll have everything—"

Luke glanced about. There was a large tin bath by the fireplace, and despite the heat of the day, someone had had the foresight to light it. The bath was full of steaming water and there were three soft towels beside it. Placed carefully upon them was a bar of what appeared to be rose soap.

It was enough.

"Thank you, that will be all," he said gruffly, slowly lowering Peggy onto the bed.

His soul cracked as she swiftly turned away.

"But I haven't finished preparing the—"

"I said that will be all, and that will be all," said Luke, temper fraying at the edges.

When he turned to apologize to the poor maid who hadn't asked to get involved in all this, she was gone.

They were alone.

"Come on, Peggy," Luke said quietly, sitting on the end of the bed. "Time for a bath."

And suddenly, before he could collect himself or resolve not to show any emotion while he was tending to the woman he loved, Peggy rushed into his arms. She clung to him, as though he were the only person alive in the world. As though he were the only one who loved her.

How long they sat there, Luke did not know. It was certainly not long enough, but then, would any amount of time ever be?

It did not take long to coax her out of her gown. Luke carefully avoided dwelling on the thought when he noticed one of her sleeves was ripped, though rage against the jape who had done such a thing sparked once more.

When Peggy was completely naked, Luke carefully lifted her once more and, paying no attention to his jacket which he swiftly threw to the carpet, placed her in the bath.

"I-I thought you had gone—"

"I'm back," said Luke gently, lifting up a sponge from the soothing water and gently drawing it over her shoulder. "And I am not going away again, Peggy. Not ever."

Did she understand him? Did she know just how sorry he was he had departed?

It would be one of the greatest regrets of his life, but it wasn't something he could explain now. Not at the moment, anyway.

"He . . . he . . . I thought he would—"

"I know," said Luke, trying his best to keep his voice level.

She was so beautiful, so fragile. What had he been thinking, leaving her alone with Castor in a place like this! Anything could have happened!

Luke's stomach turned over. *Anything almost did.*

"And I tried to stop him," said Peggy, her voice cracking as she allowed Luke to lift up a hand and gently smooth the sponge along her arm. "I-I did try, Luke—"

"You don't have to tell me about it," Luke said quietly.

In truth, the last thing he wanted was to hear about it. Hear how that brute had attempted to take what should only ever be given freely.

"I-I want to—I need you to know," Peggy gulped. "I need you to know I tried to fight him off, I didn't just let—"

And Luke's heart broke for her all over again. She thought that in some way she could be blamed for what happened? That it was in some way her fault?

"—never had to f-fight off a man before, and I-I didn't know what to do, and—"

"Peggy," Luke said over her frantic words. "Peggy, look at me."

Her dark eyes met his and his pulse skipped a beat. This woman. This wonderful woman.

"Peggy, I'm washing away all memories of that terrible man." Luke said, his voice soft but clear. "I'm washing it all away. You did nothing wrong."

Peggy's eyes were brilliantly bright, but not with tears. With something else.

"I didn't think you would understand," she whispered.

Luke tried not to reveal the pain he felt on his face.

In truth, she was right to be afraid. Oh, not of him. But there were plenty of gentlemen in the *ton* who *would* have thought she was to blame, at least in a small way, for what Castor had tried to do.

Wrong place, wrong time, of course. But why had she allowed herself to be in that place, some would whisper. And hadn't she led Castor on? Hadn't she allowed him to believe there could be something between them?

Luke tried not to growl with rage at the thoughts in his mind.

Anyone who knew anything knew men could be brutes and women were sometimes at their complete mercy. He just had to thank his lucky stars he had returned to the Sedleys' when he did.

"I understand," said Luke. "I understand that you are perfect, and—"

"Luke—"

"Will you let me finish?" he interjected with a wry smile.

Peggy's bath water was almost covered in soap bubbles now and the tension in her neck and shoulders was finally starting to melt away. *That was the power of a good bath*, Luke thought. After the very worst times in France, when he had seen things no man should ever witness, let alone suffer, it had been a long, hot bath which had washed away most of the grief and pain.

Not all of it. But most.

"I say you are perfect, and I mean it," said Luke again, pushing back a damp curl from Peggy's forehead. She smiled at his touch, and it encouraged him to go on. "What happened today— it doesn't define you. It doesn't say or mean anything about you, not at all. You are the same woman you were yesterday."

He had intended his words to be encouraging. Which did not explain the sad smile that crept across Peggy's lips.

"Not quite the same," she said quietly.

"If you want to be, you are," said Luke, taking her hand and entwining her wet fingers with his. "You are the very best thing that ever happened to me, Peggy. The best thing."

"I think I was, once," Peggy said softly, her dark eyes meeting his. "But I suppose, after everything that has happened . . . I suppose you won't want to marry me anymore."

CHAPTER EIGHTEEN

THE WORDS HAD been wrenched from her very soul as she forced herself to look at him for perhaps the last time, but Peggy knew she had to say them. Had to free him. She had fought for so long, given up so many times, but she finally had to accept that the dream she'd once had was over.

"But I suppose, after everything that has happened . . . I suppose you won't want to marry me anymore."

Luke Beauchamp, Duke of Ashcott, was not going to be her husband.

It was so clear now. Peggy could see the rest of her life stretching out before her, every day the same. Becoming the maiden aunt to Henry and Minny's children. But her life itself? That was going to be unchanging.

And . . . and that was fine. Though it mortified her to have suffered such an interaction with Castor, and to be found by the one man she had hoped would never hear of it, Peggy knew it was better this way.

They could have their goodbye today, then she would never see Luke again.

The horror on Luke's face was precisely what Peggy had expected. It was horrifying, what had happened. It was mortifying and crushing. The fact that his look of horror was so viscerally tearing into her very being was, of course, neither here nor there.

"How . . . how can you say that to me?" Luke finally said.

Peggy blinked. It was strange, having almost your exact words spoken back to you. Had she not said precisely that just a few days ago, when Luke had encouraged her to settle for Castor?

"You said Lord Castor making me happy would make you content. How can you say that?"

There was such depth of shock in Luke's expression, Peggy hardly knew what to say. "Well, I . . . I thought—"

"You thought just because something like this had happened to you, I wouldn't want to marry you?" Luke asked, eyes wide.

Peggy swallowed. *Yes,* she was going to say. *Yes, it did not even occur to me you could still want me after Castor—after all this. That after I pushed you away so many times, you would still cling to me in such a moment. That after we were separated for so long, you would even wish to come back to me at all.*

That sort of sweeping love story . . . well, it was the sort of thing that happened to Henry and Minny, wasn't it? They found each other against all the odds. It wasn't the sort of thing that happened every day.

Luke's eyes were raking over her and Peggy was a little embarrassed to see just how desirous his expression appeared.

How could he look like that at her?

"Peggy, I would never abandon you," Luke said quietly. He was still kneeling beside the tin bath, his jacket forgotten, his shirt sleeves rolled up. "You are everything—everything to me. How many times do I have to say it for you to believe me?"

Peggy tried to laugh, but somehow the sound became a sob. "I . . . I don't know!"

Words desperately crawled up her throat but she could not untangle them from each other. How could she explain her affection for him? After he had been everything to her, then absent, then a cruel mockery of what could have been, and her love again—how could she capture in just a few words what Luke was to her?

It appeared, however, that she did not need to speak. Without saying a word, Luke helped her rise from the bath. As she stood, wordless and unclothed yet more comfortable in his presence than she had ever been in her life, he slowly dried her off with the towels the maid had left.

She would have presumed this would be a sensual experience, and in a way it was. But Luke was not attempting to seduce her in this moment.

He was just loving her.

There was a large dressing gown hanging on the back of the guest bedchamber door. Peggy had only used it once, when she had slipped down early one morning for a cup of tea from the kitchen. The maids there had been scandalized and she had never done it again. Apparently what was common enough at home was rather improper here.

Now she was wearing it again. Luke had helped her slip her hands through the sleeves, then led her back to the bed. Peggy leaned back against the pillows which had been propped up against the bedhead and tried to think.

Thinking hurt.

So instead, she simply looked at Luke. He was standing beside the bed, as though unsure what he should do next. A sudden panic that he would leave washed over her, dulling all her senses and making it obvious what she had to say.

Such a shame it came out so piteously. "Please, Luke. P-Please don't leave me."

In a rush, Luke stepped around the bed and clambered onto it, sitting cross legged as he reached for her hand.

"I'm never going to leave you, Peg," he said, meeting her gaze unflinchingly. "And I think it's high time I told you a few things."

Uncertainty curled around her. What could Luke say to her? He had said he wouldn't abandon her, but that was not the same thing as wanting to be with her. It didn't mean he was ready to stay with her for the rest of his life. After the day she'd had, Peggy wasn't sure whether she wanted to hear whatever he had to say next.

Then a memory, sharp and fresh, soared into her mind. A memory of words Luke had spoken only an hour or so ago. Words that had surprised her at the time but had drifted from her focus as there had been so many other things to think on.

"I think you'll find that any lies you spread about my wife will be met with very severely, either by lawyer or by pistol."

His wife. Peggy could not understand it. Luke had not spoken to her about—

"Peggy," Luke said seriously, squeezing her hand. "I am so sorry I disappeared from your home last year when your brother . . . when I had the chance to ask permission for your hand."

And a tight band which had been encircling her, so tight Peggy had almost not noticed it was still there, suddenly released.

She gasped. How had she never noticed just what a grip that moment had on her heart? Only now it was gone could she see how painful it had been. How it had constricted her, refrained her from loving in the way she had wanted.

In the way she and Luke deserved.

"And I am sorry I did not come back the next day," Luke continued doggedly, as though now that he had started he had to get the whole speech out. "Or the next day. By the third day I had already gone to France—"

"To serve your country," Peggy pointed out, desperately trying to remember that. "Without your argument with my brother—"

"Your brother was right to say those things, and I was wrong to walk away," Luke said. His hand was tight on hers. Peggy rather thought his grip could never be tight enough. "Our lives would have been different if I had just thought for a moment beyond my stubbornness, beyond my pride."

Peggy allowed herself a small smile as her stomach turned over. "I think we have those faults in common."

He laughed dryly, shaking his head. "I never thought I would say this but . . . well, I have something to show you."

Peggy frowned as Luke clambered off the bed to retrieve his jacket from the carpet. "What could you have in there?"

"Something I have carried around with me for far too long," said Luke.

For a moment as Luke climbed back onto the bed to sit beside her, Peggy allowed herself to hope—

Well, it wasn't her fault, was it? An engagement ring was a fad to be sure, and half those she spoke to of it in Town believed the fashion would be over in a few years. Offering a woman a ring, preferably with a few gemstones, just to prove you wished to be married? Extravagance!

Still. Peggy had permitted herself, just a few times in the last year, to dream. Dream of a Luke who returned with all these sorts of apologies. All these declarations of love. And then he would reach into a pocket of his jacket and out would come a box. A jewelry box. And inside it would be an extravagance indeed.

Peggy's breath caught in her throat as Luke's hand rummaged in a pocket, but she was careful not to permit herself a sigh of disappointment as he pulled out not a ring box, but a piece of paper.

A crumpled, much folded, slightly stained piece of paper.

"Ah," said Peggy lightly, as though she had hardly cared what Luke had to show her. "A piece of paper."

"It's a letter," Luke said ruefully. "A letter I wrote, and have added to, and amended, almost continuously this last year."

Her curiosity rose. A letter? Clearly one he thought important, otherwise why else continue to amend it, improve it. But then why not send it?

"A letter," she repeated.

Peggy gasped as Luke's devoted expression lifted from the paper to her.

"A letter to you," he said softly. "A letter I was always afraid to send. A letter I knew would never truly capture everything I felt about you, and the more I tried to improve it—Peggy!"

He was laughing, thank goodness. Heat burned Peggy's cheeks as she withdrew the hand which had reached forward unconsciously.

"Well, it's for me, isn't it?" she said defensively, trying to pretend it was completely natural she had attempted to take the letter from his hands. "Don't you want me to read it?"

Peggy looked up at Luke's face.

They had survived so much—though in many cases, just barely. It had been so hard to believe this could happen at all. That they would find each other again.

Luke's smile was a bit wry. "Once you read this, you may think less of me."

"I doubt that," Peggy said, twisting to face him better on the bed.

All thoughts of what had happened with Castor, that she was naked underneath this robe, that all the houseguests below must be speculating wildly about what they were doing up here, alone . . . all those concerns melted away.

She was precisely where she needed to be. With Luke.

"Why don't I read it to you, then?" suggested Luke. "That way I can—"

"Leave out the parts you think I won't like?" teased Peggy.

Something in her altered as she spoke. Shifted in her, as though she were becoming herself again. As though what Castor had tried to take from her was still within her. He had failed. And she'd won.

Luke's eyes glittered. "Exactly. After all, I've amended it enough times. I suppose I can adjust it again as we go."

Peggy tried once more to pluck the letter from his hands, but once again his reflexes were superior.

"Are you going to listen or not?" he asked sternly.

Something delicious overcame her, and before she knew what she was saying, Peggy raised an eyebrow. "What will you do to me if I don't?"

Luke groaned and moved a few inches away. "You are incorrigible, Peggy Everleigh!"

"I should hope so," said Peggy, excitement pooling in her stomach. There was something about seeing the effect of her words on Luke. Something that promised of more delights to come.

"Right, here we go," said Luke, clearing his voice. "My darling Peggy—"

"Darling? I don't think you've called me darling in your entire life!" interrupted Peggy, eagerness making it impossible to stay quiet.

Well, how often did she get a handsome duke reading her a love letter?

Just an hour ago, Peggy thought she would be defined forever by the disgusting things Castor had attempted to do to her. But Luke had been right. Somehow, and she did not understand how, he had washed away all memory of what had happened in the library. Everything she had feared, all the pain she had felt. It had washed away. She felt renewed, newly alive in his presence.

Even if he was glaring with mock severity. "Will you let me read this letter or not?"

"Yes, yes, fine," said Peggy, meekly folding her hands in her lap and gazing up as though butter wouldn't melt.

A jolt through her body sparked tendrils of pleasure at his look. *Well. He would melt butter.*

"As I was saying," Luke said, flourishing the piece of paper again. "My darling Peggy, it seems an age since I have seen you last—"

"It was indeed."

"Peggy!"

"Sorry," said Peggy hastily, smiling to see his mock outrage. "I truly will try to listen."

"I'll believe that when I—"

"Luke!"

"Sorry," he shot back with a grin. "Now, where was I?"

"I think you were about to launch into a description of my beauty," said Peggy with a laugh, leaning back on the pillows, and wondering how she could ever stop loving this man.

Luke's eyes widened and his cheeks pinked. "How did you know that?"

Peggy laughed. *How would she ever grow truly accustomed to Luke Beauchamp?* "Fortunate guess."

He was frowning, just a hint of embarrassment evident on his face. "Fine. Well . . . well, I say something complimentary and then—"

"Luke!"

"Fine, I'll read it out—but you have to promise not to laugh." Luke took a deep breath, and it was only then she realized just what a difficult task this was for him.

Here was a man raised to be silent on his finer emotions. To pretend, in effect, they did not exist. And now here he was, reading his innermost thoughts to her. Thoughts he never intended for her to see, let alone hear from his own mouth. He was one of the bravest men she had ever met.

Luke cleared his throat. "It seems an age since I have seen you last, but the memory of your beauty has not faded. I can still see the way you laugh, the glint in your eye as you challenge me. I've never been more entertained and more defied than when in your presence, and . . . and now I am apart from you, I weep to think I may never be with you again."

Peggy stared, transfixed. These were such words as she had longed to hear from Luke's lips—except they were far more wonderful, far deeper and more vulnerable than she could have imagined.

"Losing you was the greatest mistake of my life, and though I am not even halfway through it, I know I shall never regret anything more," Luke continued, reading from the paper with pink cheeks. "I . . . I know you will never forgive me, and knowing myself barred from you is agony. My friends are tired of hearing about you—"

"Luke!" Peggy exclaimed, unable to help herself. Had he really spoken to his friends about her?

"—tired of hearing about you, and I can't blame them," Luke read with another wry smile. "They, like me, cannot bear to think this could be the rest of my life. All I know is that I will have to spend the rest of my days working to deserve you. Not because you are owed to me, but because even if I never speak to you again, I wish to live a life . . . a life worthy of you. There. That's it."

He folded the letter and placed it on the bed, only lifting his eyes to her after taking a deep breath, as though preparing himself for the worst.

"I can't believe you wrote those words," said Peggy hoarsely. It was a wonder she could speak at all.

"I can't believe I didn't send it," said Luke remorsefully. "I was afraid—afraid you wouldn't appreciate seeing it. Afraid you might just throw it away or burn it before even reading it. But I knew that if I were ever to see you again, really see you, and capture your heart again—"

"I can't believe you doubted it."

"—I knew I would need to have something other than a scrap of paper," Luke said quietly.

Peggy opened her mouth to speak, then closed it again. There was something in the way he had said that. Something vulnerable, which was not a word she readily associated with Luke. Something told her what he was about to say was neither flippant, nor jesting. He was about to be very serious.

"And . . . and what was that?" she asked curiously.

Peggy watched as Luke reached once more into his jacket, and pulled out—

Her jaw fell open. "That—that's—"

"Why did you think I left?" asked Luke softly as he turned the small blue velvet box over and over between his fingers. "Do you think anything else would have convinced me to part from you so soon after we had reconciled? How could I do such a thing, unless

I was going to buy . . ."

"It's not," Peggy whispered. "Is it?"

It was all too much. As Luke slowly opened up the box to reveal an elegant golden band with three pearls, one beside the other, Peggy saw not the value of the ring but something far more precious.

A promise.

"Three pearls," she said quietly.

"One for you," Luke said softly. "One for me."

She could hardly breathe. *And the third?*

As though he had heard her unspoken question, Luke brushed his thumb over the three pearls. "And one for the future. For the beauty of what we will create together. For all the times we may not understand each other, but as long as we have love—"

"We'll have love," said Peggy, lifting her gaze from the box to the man offering it to her. "We'll always have love."

Luke breathed an awkward laugh. "I hope so."

"I know so," Peggy said firmly.

How she could be so certain, she did not know. All she knew was that after suffering so much apart, they could only be happy when they were together.

"I suppose the only thing remaining," Peggy said slowly, "is to ask you to marry me."

Luke's eyes widened in shock and he moved closer. "No—no, I am supposed to—"

"Well, too late now," said Peggy briskly, trying not to laugh openly. *Oh, this man.* "I got there first. Now, what is your answer."

"No."

Her face fell. *What the—*

"Now," said Luke. "Will you marry me?"

Peggy did not need to answer with words. Launching herself at Luke so swiftly he dropped the jewelry box, their heady kiss was more than enough to seal the bargain they had wordlessly made.

She trembled in his arms. His passion was unrestrained, his kisses sparking bliss down her neck and toward her breasts, and she knew she wanted more. All of him. To know him even better than she did now. To know him better tomorrow than she ever would today.

The kiss lasted far longer than she expected and was over too swiftly.

"Well," said Luke with a deep breath. "Time to get dressed."

Peggy looked up with lust hazed eyes. *Dressed? At a time like this?* "Whatever for?"

"Because I think there are a few people downstairs who want to know what's going on," said Luke dryly. "I believe I may owe them an explanation for ordering a bath, taking you up here, and not reappearing for . . . goodness, I couldn't even tell you how long."

Peggy pulled the man she loved closer for another kiss. "Let them wonder. Just for another hour . . ."

CHAPTER NINETEEN

5 September, 1811

"AND FESTOONS OF blue roses," Luke said happily, lying on a blanket in the dying sunlight. "And orange roses! And violets, and—ouch! That hurt!"

"It was supposed to," came a calm and dignified voice just to his left. "Be serious, Luke!"

He sat up with a grin, heart glowing to see Peggy glaring so defiantly. "Serious? I am serious."

"Blue roses? You know they simply do not exist," said Peggy quellingly, glancing at the list spooling across her lap and over the rug. "And even if they did exist, with orange roses? The clash of the colors, it simply wouldn't—"

"I like orange," said Luke. "And violet. And—"

"If you are not careful, I shall throw another cushion," Peggy warned. "And then I'll have run out of cushions, and I'll have to throw something else!"

Luke breathed in deeply as he looked at the woman he loved.

It had been her idea to come out here. Oh, the Dulverton house was all very well. It was elegantly furnished, as one would expect the residence of a duke to be. It was almost welcoming. And the Duchess of Dulverton did her best, but nothing could entirely defrost the icy glances from her husband.

His stomach lurched. *Well, Peggy's brother was hardly going to be the most enthusiastic about the announcement.*

And so, after a rather frosty ten minutes of sipping scalding tea in the drawing room, Peggy had suggested she and Luke go sit in the garden to discuss the last few details of the wedding. The Duchess of Dulverton had swiftly agreed, and that had been that.

Luke propped himself up on an elbow as he looked at his future bride.

Peggy Everleigh. He would never truly understand what he had done to deserve her, and in a way, he was rather glad he didn't. If he knew what he'd done right, there was a chance he could mess it up again.

His gaze meandered over the last of the summer blooms, brilliant in the flower beds, to Peggy who was running through what appeared to be the world's longest checklist.

"You do know we're just getting married," Luke pointed out lazily. *Goodness, it was still so warm.* "Not invading a small country."

"We may as well be, the amount of food Cook will be preparing," Peggy muttered under her breath.

Luke snorted. "I hadn't realized planning a wedding was such a kerfuffle!"

"Neither did I," said Peggy, pushing back a strand of hair without looking up. "If my brother hadn't been so unhelpful as to elope, then I would have at least had some practice."

A frown settled across Luke's brow. *Eloped?*

Now that was a story he'd not heard before. He had just presumed he'd not been invited to the Dulverton wedding because he was, at the time, persona non grata. Sometimes when he came to visit now, and Dulverton looked at him as though he'd like to tear him in three pieces, he still felt that way.

But if the man had truly eloped—well, Peggy's brother didn't have a leg to stand on when it came to criticizing their own plans. Which he had done only slightly, Luke would admit. But still. He had done it.

"Well, they say practice makes perfect," Luke said with a laugh. "And as this is the second time that we've been engaged—"

Peggy looked up with a half-exasperated, half-amused expression. "If you are not careful, my lad, we will be testing out the adage of 'third time's the charm,' so don't ruin this one!"

Luke snorted and was rewarded with a beaming smile from Peggy.

That was one of the things he loved about her so much. Not that she did not get angry—everyone had the right to get angry at some point, though he did so perhaps more often than he should. No, it was that even after he had made her furious, she was always willing to forgive him. And that was something far more precious than the pearl and gold ring on the fourth finger of her left hand.

His stomach jolted. That always happened whenever Luke looked at that ring. It was a statement of fact: that he loved her, and that she loved him enough to wear it. She may not bear his name yet, nor his crest, but this was the first step to that journey. The best journey he would ever take in his life.

"Third time's the charm, indeed," he murmured.

"It's what they say," said Peggy, who had returned to her list. "We didn't hear back from Lady Romeril, did we?"

"She'll arrive anyway and act astonished if we try to tell her she did not reply to our invitation," Luke said dryly. "Mark her as attending."

"I seem to have marked everyone as attending," said Peggy slowly, running her finger down another list which she picked up carefully. "I had no idea you were so popular in Society, Luke. These people can't be coming for me."

Luke swallowed.

Well, of course they were, he wanted to say. *For both of us.* It had turned out that Peggy had been quite right—there had been plenty of gossip in the scandal sheets when it had all came crashing down. Now everyone wanted to see precisely what the reconciliation looked like.

He couldn't blame them. He personally was appreciating his front row seat.

"And the Penshaws are coming," said Peggy vaguely. "And the Martocks. I haven't heard from—"

"I can't believe it's finally happening," said Luke, words spilling from his lips as a gentle breeze rustled past. "After losing you."

There must have been something pitiful in his tone, for at his words, Peggy looked up. "You never truly lost me, you know."

Luke wanted to believe her. It was most gratifying to think that all those months, she had never ceased to care for him.

Her smile was affectionate and she reached out to cup his cheek, just for a moment. "You'll never escape me now."

"I should never have lost you in the first place," said Luke, more seriously than he had intended.

But Peggy was smiling, beside him on the rug, and no one had come out to disturb them or ensure they weren't doing what he greatly wished to be doing. Doing the one thing they had agreed they would not do, once their engagement had been made official.

They had only slipped up . . . what, twice?

"You're a duke," said Peggy, "but you had no idea how to talk to my brother. You had no manners."

Luke sat up hastily at that. "No manners?"

"None whatsoever," Peggy said, her eyes dancing. "And you were all the more attractive for it. You think I would have attached myself so utterly to a man who lived up to the expectations of the *ton*?"

Luke stared, pushing his hair from his eyes as he tried to comprehend what she was saying. "I had a terrible reputation in Society, I know that. Have, rather."

"Yes, as a rake, a rogue, a seducer," said Peggy, glancing again at her list. "Why did you think I was so intrigued?"

By God! All this time, Luke had presumed he had made Peggy

Everleigh fall in love with him despite his terrible reputation. But now she was saying that it was, in some small way, because of it? It was all he could do not to wrench the list from her hand and make her explain.

"You astonish me," he managed to say.

A gentle laugh escaped Peggy's lips. "I am afraid you may have to get used to that. I intend to astonish you every day for the rest of our lives."

Their laughter filled the garden, and Luke fought against the impulse to pull her into his arms and kiss her rotten.

Oh, the things she could do to him.

"Well, perhaps it is a good thing we had a little time apart," said Luke with a sigh, leaning back to look up at the sky. "Perhaps you would have always wondered what your life would have been without me, unless we had experienced a taste."

He had thought her absorbed once more in the never-ending lists, so was surprised to see Peggy's face appear above him.

Her expression was solemn and her voice quavered as she spoke. "But Luke, if—if anything had happened to you. Something awful, I mean. In France."

Luke's breathing halted, just for a moment. It was a frightening thought. He had been a green-gilled fool going out there just to escape his complicated feelings for a woman he had thought barred from him. Nothing could have prepared him well enough, but he'd truly had no idea whatsoever.

Everything could have been very different.

"I would never have forgiven myself, you know," said Peggy softly.

She was pressed up against him now, seated beside him with a hand placed on his chest. A few curls, escaping their pins, fell toward him.

Peggy, never forgiving herself?

"It wouldn't have been your fault," he said gruffly. He could hardly bear to think about it. "It was my fault, we've been over this—"

"I could have gone after you," Peggy said earnestly. "I could have—"

"No one wins this sort of game," said Luke, trying not to think about what could have been. "Which reminds me. Lord Castor has officially emigrated."

"Emigrated?"

"To America."

Peggy looked absolutely astonished—as well she might, Luke thought. The news had not reached the scandal sheets yet . . . but it would.

"America?" repeated his bride-to-be. "Are you certain?"

Luke tried not to think about the lengths he had gone to procuring passage, the letters between him and Sedley, the inscription of the destination on the paperwork. New York. "Very certain."

"And he'll never come back—"

"Look, all of that is in the past and I suggest we leave it there," said Luke, sitting up and kissing Peggy swiftly on the lips. "I don't want to be raking it up all the time. We love each other. We're here. Let's think about the future."

Was that a knowing look in his future wife's eye?

"Excellent," said Peggy brightly. She pulled something between them.

Luke looked down and groaned. *That damned list!*

"Now, I want this wedding to be perfect," Peggy said with worrying determination, "So we need to make a few decisions. Where are we going to live once we are married?"

Luke blinked. "Why, in my townhouse of course."

"Not in the country?" she asked, glancing around. "I think being at the Sedleys' reminded me of just how much I like the country."

Entirely bewildered, and not sure precisely what this had to do with their wedding, Luke shrugged. "Whatever will make you happiest. I have a seat in Devon. It's wonderful."

"It is?" Peggy's eyes shone.

Luke reached up and tucked a curl behind her ear, marveling at the softness of her skin, the way he constantly wished to be ripping off her gowns rather than allowing her to continue scandalously clothed.

"Ashcott Hall is perhaps not as large as the Sedleys' place," he began.

Peggy snorted. "Good. I was constantly getting lost!"

"It does have a ballroom though," Luke admitted. *Well, it was best to get the worst over with.*

"Excellent."

Luke blinked. "I thought you just said—"

"Well, when we host our own house parties, it would be nice to have a ball, don't you think?" said Peggy with a smile. "And a library, we must have a large one. And the stables—"

"I am not changing my stables for you or for anyone," Luke said resolutely. "Nor my lake."

Apparently he had managed to say the right thing. "You do have stables then? And a lake, you say?"

Luke laughed with a wry shake of his head. "Are you marrying my lake or me?"

Peggy grinned. "Well, now that I know you have a lake—"

"Peg!"

"Fine, fine. Now, we need to decide who we will be inviting first to stay."

Luke stared. None of this made any sense. He had presumed she would wish to discuss guest lists, the schedule of their wedding day, just how much wine had to be ordered now they had agreed Lady Romeril was coming, not preparing for houseguests for future parties!

"I don't—"

"Because I think really, we should invite the Sedleys, even if I have to put up with those terrible eggs," said Peggy thoughtfully. "They were so kind to us, you know. And Lord Braedon—"

"I am not hosting Viscount Braedon, no matter how charming you may think he is," Luke said. "The man's a menace!"

"Only to himself," Peggy giggled.

He shrugged, unable to argue with her on that one.

"Well, if we don't have Lord Braedon, I wondered what you thought of—"

"Peggy," interrupted Luke, unable to help himself. "I don't understand."

She looked as perplexed it appeared as he felt. "What don't you understand?"

"I thought we were wedding planning," said Luke awkwardly. *Well, it was not as though he was an expert.* "But all of these details—where we'll live, what we'll do with our time, who we'll see—that's all about our marriage. Not the wedding."

Her eyes flashed for a moment, and once again Luke recalled what had drawn him to this wonderful woman from across the room at Almack's.

It wasn't her beauty. Oh, her beauty didn't hurt, but it wasn't that. It was the way she held herself. The absolute certainty that no matter what Peggy was doing, it was the right thing to do. There was something intoxicating about that sort of conviction.

"Luke Beauchamp, Duke of Ashcott," Peggy said quietly, "I'm not marrying you for the wedding. I'm marrying you to be your wife. To build a life together, a life full of laughter, and love, and friends—"

"And family?" groaned Luke with an exaggerated sigh, thinking of his future brother-in-law.

She poked him with a finger. "And family. Because I want everything with you, Luke. I want to share it all. All of it."

Luke's heart twisted. "I do love you, Peg."

"And I love you, Luke," she said, and he could see how much she meant it.

Their kiss was swift. The windows of the drawing room looked out over the garden, and you could never quite tell who was watching. But in that moment, when their minds were so attuned with each other, Luke absolutely knew he had to kiss her.

It was over almost as soon as it had begun. His need for her—

his craving—was unsated, but it would have to be for some time. Until the wedding. Until their wedding night.

Peggy sighed with what appeared to be complete happiness. "Do you think other people feel this content?"

Luke's hands tightened on hers. "I hope they do. I hope everyone can find something of what we have found with each other."

"And my brother? You know how he feels about you. Can you be content with that?"

Though he hesitated only for a moment, Luke could see that Peggy had noticed. "Not every family is perfect. In fact, I would hazard a guess none are. So, your brother doesn't like me."

"Well—"

"Doesn't like me," reiterated Luke with a chuckle. "As long as he does not object at our wedding—"

Peggy's eyes widened. "You don't think he would—"

"—then I'll have everything I need right here," said Luke, putting an arm around her waist.

She did not resist. Luke's whole being leapt as their lips met, her tongue eagerly reaching for his own, the little whimper of pleasure making him deepen the kiss and—

"Put my sister down or marry her this afternoon, you heathen!"

Luke groaned as he pulled away from Peggy. "Damn."

"Ignore him," murmured Peggy, cheeks scarlet. "He's just—"

"He's your brother, and until you are my wife, I suppose I will have to listen, at least a little, to what he says," said Luke regretfully. *Damn it.* "This wedding, this marriage . . . it cannot come soon enough."

EPILOGUE

21 September, 1811

PEGGY PULLED DISTRACTEDLY at her veil. It wasn't straight. She didn't need to see it to know it. She could feel it. Something wasn't right.

"Are you sure?" said a voice with a glower behind her. "There's still time."

A smile slipped across Peggy's face as she turned on her heel, squeaking on the marble of their hallway.

His hallway. In an hour or so, this place would cease to be her home.

Her brother, Henry, was frowning. "I mean it. You say the word and I can call this whole thing off. No one will ever mention it again. You can just go. We'll go into the country. Or Italy, I hear it's lovely—"

"Henry," said Peggy softly.

"There's no shame in realizing you've made a bad decision," he said fiercely, taking a step toward her. He was attired in his very best and most uncomfortable suit, which could not be improving his mood. "Leave him at the altar, I say—"

"Henry," she said again.

"—because whatever you say, I'll do, Peg. Even if it means

causing upset," Henry said, his face set. "You're my sister. And I won't allow you to do something you might regret, just because you're worried about—"

"Henry," Peggy said, taking his hands in hers. "I *want* to marry him."

Henry glared. "You do?"

Peggy sighed.

She did. Even after everything they had been through. After all the misunderstandings. The love and affection which seemed lost. The joy she had found, then lost, then found, then lost—she wouldn't have it any other way. She wouldn't want a life with anyone who could not be him. Luke Beauchamp, Duke of Ashcott.

"I love him," Peggy reminded her brother.

Henry snorted. "Love."

"You married for love," she pointed out, glancing over at her sister-in-law. Minny had just entered the hallway in a resplendent pink gown, all lace edging and gold thread. "You married the woman you adored."

"I married the person I could not do without," said Henry stiffly, as his wife slipped her hand around his arm. "But you, on the other hand—"

"You are marrying the man you cannot do without," said Minny cheerfully, beaming at Peggy. "I've seen the way you look at him. And the way he looks at you."

"Minny!"

"Well!" she said with a laugh at her husband. "I don't think there's time to talk her out of it, Henry. The pair of them are besotted with each other!"

Peggy flushed and dropped her brother's hands.

She had thought—well, hoped—no one had noticed. But apparently it was quite clear she and Luke could not wait to be married.

They had tried to be good. And they had, in the main.

But as Luke had said only two days ago, it was blessed frustrating to have to wait to make love again until they were technically husband and wife. Just a few more hours . . .

"You look nervous."

Henry's pointed remark made Peggy smile. "You're making me nervous, Henry."

"Aha!"

"Because you won't stop bothering me," she added, rolling her eyes at her ridiculous brother. "This is my wedding day! It's meant to be all festivities, and light, and—"

"And it will be," said Minny firmly. "I am sure of that. *We're* sure—aren't we, Henry?"

Peggy tried not to laugh as she watched her brother be nudged, rather violently, by his wife, even with a now slightly swollen stomach full of a growing child.

"Fine," said Henry heavily, shaking his head. "Minny, go out to the carriage, will you? I need a word with my sister. Don't worry, I'll be gentle," he added, after seeing her face.

Minny leaned up and kissed him before beaming at Peggy. "Just don't be too long, Henry. Brides are supposed to be late, but we're pushing it a bit fine here!"

The door closed behind her and Peggy looked at her brother.

Well, she had expected this, she thought as she tugged her veil. *Why wasn't it straight?*

Henry had made it perfectly clear, the last few weeks, that he was accepting Luke's suit under advisement. Peggy's advisement. For no other reason was he tolerating it. And she had known Henry would need to have one final conversation with her. Just to make sure, as he would put it. To give her another opportunity to let Luke slip through her fingers.

"Peg," said Henry heavily.

Peggy set her face for this unwelcome monologue.

Henry sighed. "I am sorry."

Peggy blinked. She must have heard that incorrectly. She could not have heard that right, could she? *Henry, apologize?*

"I can see you love the devil—"

"Henry!"

"Old habits die hard," her brother said with a rueful grin. "But seriously, Peg. I see the way you look at him."

Panic began to play at the edges of her awareness. The last thing she needed was her brother guessing that she and Luke—

"And I see the way he looks at you," Henry continued, his voice softer now. "Adoration. Minny's right, he is besotted with you."

Peggy looked up and met her brother's eyes. They were glittering with tears.

"I never thought I'd meet anyone who I liked enough for you," Henry admitted with a sigh. "And I think this whole scenario has proven that . . . that I don't have to."

Peggy frowned. "You don't have to?"

Henry shrugged. "It's not up to me to like him. I don't have to live with the scoundrel. It's you. Your opinion, I mean, that matters."

Delight replaced panic and continued to spread through Peggy as she took in her brother's words.

"And I am sorry," her brother added wryly, "for ruining it in the first place."

Peggy breathed a laugh as she stepped forward and pulled him into an embrace. "You silly man."

"I am indeed," said Henry with a laugh. "And I think in many ways, I'll continue silly. But it shouldn't ruin your happiness, Peg. I shouldn't. I hope you know that."

She squeezed her well-meaning and entirely misguided brother with a sigh of relief.

She hadn't known precisely what was wrong. She had thought it was the veil most of the morning—but now she knew. It was Henry. Without his blessing, without knowing she had his support, the whole day would have felt . . . wrong, somehow. Now she had it.

"I forgive you, Henry," Peggy said. "But not for setting Miss Yates onto me."

Henry tightened his grip, just for a moment, then stepped back and dashed a wayward tear from his eyes. "Ah. You worked that out, then?"

Peggy poked her brother, hard, in the chest. "What on earth were you thinking?"

"Thinking of you, of course!" he said defensively. "There you were, off to a house party without a chaperone or a single friend—"

"If you'd just told me, I could have been more open with Miss Yates from the start," Peggy pointed out with a laugh. "Then you would have got your news from the horse's mouth."

Henry's face was a picture of astonishment. "Oh. I didn't think of that."

Peggy laughed. Well, there was no changing some people— and her brother would insist on trying to take care of her, whether he should or not.

"Lord above, we're late."

"We are late," said Peggy with a laugh. "Over a year late, if you ask me. But I'm certain Luke will be waiting."

Henry gave her a look, then offered her his arm. "Yes. You know, I think he will."

And he was. Peggy had been unable to settle throughout the entire carriage ride to the church, the sound of bells growing louder and louder the closer they grew. And when the church doors opened, and she and Henry started to walk up the aisle, there was only one face she sought.

Luke.

Peggy's heart skipped a beat. He was so handsome—and not just handsome, but good. And not just good, but kind. And not just kind, but strong, strong enough to protect her and love her and challenge her for the rest of their days.

By the time she and Henry reached the top of the nave, her legs felt a little shaky and Peggy was relieved that she had her brother's arm to lean on.

But not for much longer.

"Who gives this woman to this man?" asked the vicar.

Peggy's gaze flickered between the two men who meant so much to her. The only two men in the world she truly loved. The two men in her life who would acclimatize to each other, even if it took a lifetime.

And Henry was smiling. It was a stiff smile, admittedly. But it was a smile, nonetheless.

"I do," Henry said clearly. Then he dropped his voice. "And if you don't care for her well, you rogue, I'll make sure it's the very last thing you ever—"

"Yes, thank you, Henry," Peggy said hastily, pushing her brother aside and taking her place beside Luke.

Honestly! The man had no self-control!

Luke was grinning. "Glad to see some things never change."

"Some things do," Peggy breathed, glancing at the vicar who was holding a golden band and looking a bit bemused at the exchange. "My name, for a start."

The vows passed by so quickly she could hardly take notice of them. She had thought she would remember every single moment precisely, that the whole event would be perfectly preserved in her mind like a flower pressed between two pages.

But she blinked and Luke was leading her down the aisle between their adoring friends and relations, a golden band on her finger.

"Good afternoon, Peggy Beauchamp," said Luke softly as they stepped over the church threshold.

Peggy was not sure if he had expected her to launch herself into his arms like that, but Luke recovered very quickly. To the evident horror of those gasping behind them, she kissed her husband passionately on the mouth, and reveled in the way she could do so now without any fear that he would be taken from her.

She had done it. Finally, she had married one of the most scandalous rakes in all the *ton*.

"My word!"

"I say!"

"The audacity!"

Peggy was grinning as she broke the kiss, and her smile only widened as she saw Luke's bashful smile.

"What was that for?"

"For you, of course," she said serenely. "And if we didn't have to celebrate the wedding reception, you know precisely where I would want to take you."

Luke's dark eyes flashed with mischief. "My townhouse does have a small kitchen garden, actually."

A stir of longing ached between Peggy's legs. Perhaps—

"Come on, you two!" said Minny with a laugh. "We're hosting the reception, and as the guests of honor, we can't start without you!"

Peggy supposed it was because of her brother's own scandalous wedding that he and Minny had decided to be so extravagant. If they had not eloped to Gretna Green, making it impossible for her or anyone else in Society to attend, perhaps they would not have gone to such trouble.

"My goodness!" boomed Lady Romeril as she entered the saloon in the Dulverton household. "What on earth is this?"

Peggy had to admit, it was rather spectacular.

The saloon was always splendidly decorated, with more gold paneling and mirrors than any room had a right to contain. But then there were the plethora of candles and the way elegant console tables had been placed around the room and all other furniture removed to give the illusion of almost unlimited space. The musicians, seated in one corner playing something that sounded like Mozart. And the food—

"Only the very best for my sister," Henry said stiffly, coming up to Peggy and Luke as they stood, mouths gaping in awe. "The very best."

"*I* heard the very best things in life were dukes," Luke murmured in her ear.

Peggy expected her cheeks to flush, but they did not. Perhaps being a married woman made her impervious to such things.

"Ashcott," said Henry formally.

And then he did something Peggy could never have expected.

He held out his hand.

For a terrifying moment, she thought Luke would not accept the tacit apology—but then her husband reached out and grasped the hand of her brother.

"Dulverton," he said quietly.

Peggy could hardly believe it. *What else was going to happen?* The rest of the wedding party seemed to be occurring without them, utterly oblivious to the fact that such strides had been made.

"Well, I'd better shout at a footman, or something," Henry said vaguely, dropping Luke's hand. "Later, Ashcott."

"Dulverton," said Luke, inclining his head. Only when his new brother-in-law had stepped over six feet away did he drop his voice and whisper in Peggy's ear. "He's not really going to shout at a footman, is he?"

"Henry? I doubt he's shouted in his entire life," Peggy said dryly. "Even when he threw you out of the house, he was remarkably restrained. Didn't you think?"

"I try not to think about that moment in my life too much," Luke said with a wry smile. "Besides, I've made so many good memories today alone. I have far more pleasant things to think on."

Peggy squeezed his arm. He was right. Whatever pain they had shared in the past, it was in the past. All they had to do was create new memories.

"It looks like the whole of Society decided to attend," she said, glancing around them. "I thought the Sedleys would be here."

"Not if Her Grace is still feeling the effects of the pregnancy which hasn't been announced," he said with a wink.

Peggy's stomach lurched. Was now the right time? He had said before, hadn't he, that he wouldn't announce before the quickening?

But an announcement wasn't the same as telling the father was it?

"What is wrong?" Luke said. His face was a picture of concern. "Peg? You suddenly went all pale, are you quite well?"

"I . . . I think," Peggy said delicately, "that it may be a good idea for us to take tea with the Sedleys. Soon."

Her husband was frowning. "What on earth for?"

"For a little advice," Peggy said slowly, looking deep into his eyes. "About . . . about the early stages of—"

She was left unable to complete her sentence. A very sudden embrace will do that to a woman.

"Peggy Everleigh!" Luke cried, much to the consternation of their guests. "You—you're not—"

"If you don't release me this moment, the entirety of the *ton* will know!" Peggy wheezed.

He had the grace to look a little apologetic as he stepped back. "I just—"

"I know," said Peggy. "But until we have spoken to a doctor, we should probably not—"

"Yes, right," said Luke, a dazed expression now on his face. "Goodness. Right."

Peggy shook her head ruefully. "Every single person in your acquaintance is going to be asking you about that ridiculous display, you know."

Luke sighed with far more sadness than Peggy had expected. "Except Chetnole."

Ah. Of course. Peggy had become so wrapped up in her own happy beginnings, she had quite forgotten that for a friend of her new husband's, it may be more about endings.

"Nothing has been heard?"

"No one has seen hide nor hair of him in France or in England," said Luke heavily. "You wouldn't think a duke could just disappear into thin air, would you?"

"We could help with the search effort," Peggy said quietly. How, precisely, she was not certain—but if her estimation that

Luke had secretly been a spy in France was correct, he would have a fair idea.

The look in his eyes suggested she was correct. "Perhaps. We should start with Kent. If there was any way that he could get over the Channel—"

"Perhaps we can think about it tomorrow," Peggy said with a smile. "I know the best things in life are dukes—"

"My word, should I be jealous?" teased Luke, dropping her hand but instead circling his arm around her waist, in full view of the room at large. "Do I have a rival to be concerned about?"

Peggy beamed up into the mischievous eyes of the man she loved. The man who had proven, time and time again, he would be faithful to her. Even if it all seemed hopeless.

"Never," she whispered. "There will never be anyone for me, Luke, but you. You, and our child."

And ignoring the scandalized gasps of those around them, Peggy leaned forward and claimed his lips for the next of a lifetime of passionate kisses.

About Emily E K Murdoch

If you love falling in love, then you've come to the right place.

I am a historian and writer and have a varied career to date: from examining medieval manuscripts to designing museum exhibitions, to working as a researcher for the BBC to working for the National Trust.

My books range from England 1050 to Texas 1848, and I can't wait for you to fall in love with my heroes and heroines!

Follow me on twitter and instagram @emilyekmurdoch, find me on facebook at facebook.com/theemilyekmurdoch, and read my blog at www.emilyekmurdoch.com.